HAYLEE AND COMET

A Tale of Cosmic Friendship

DEBORAH MARCERO

Roaring Brook Press
New York

To every friend who
dropped out of the sky
just at the moment I needed.

This book is a love letter to you. —DM

Published by Roaring Brook Press
Roaring Brook Press is a division of Holtzbrinck Publishing Holdings Limited Partnership
120 Broadway, New York, NY 10271 • mackids.com

Library of Congress Control Number: 2020918237
ISBN 978-1-250-77439-2

Our books may be purchased in bulk for promotional, educational, or business use.
Please contact your local bookseller or the Macmillan Corporate and Premium Sales Department
at (800) 221-7945 ext. 5442 or by email at MacmillanSpecialMarkets@macmillan.com.

First edition, 2021 • Book design by Kirk Benshoff

The illustrations for this book were created with ink, colored pencils, watercolor,
gouache, and acrylic paint on hot press watercolor paper.

Printed in China by Toppan Leefung Printing Ltd., Dongguan City, Guangdong Province

3 5 7 9 10 8 6 4 2

This book belongs to: Kendall Kitchen

THE
WISH

To Haylee, wishes were magic.
She made one every chance she could.

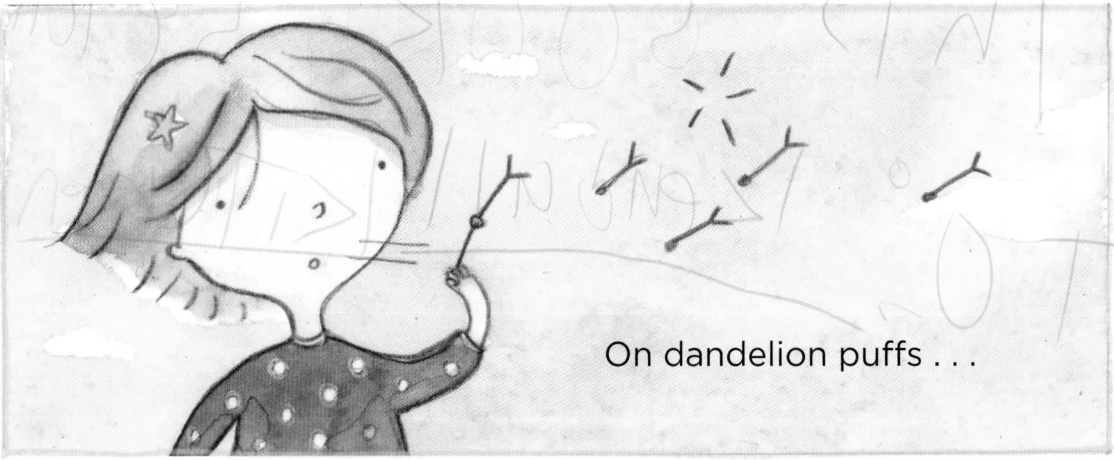
On dandelion puffs . . .

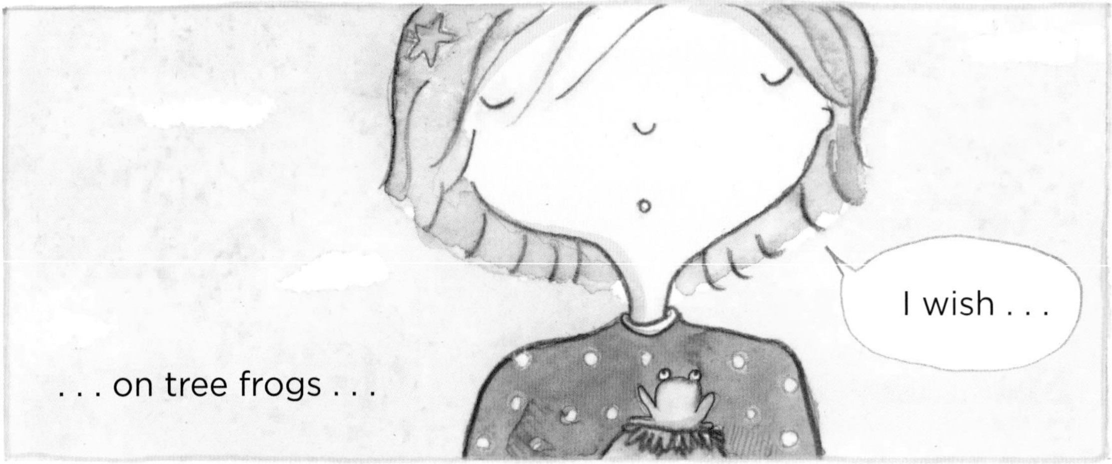
I wish . . .
. . . on tree frogs . . .

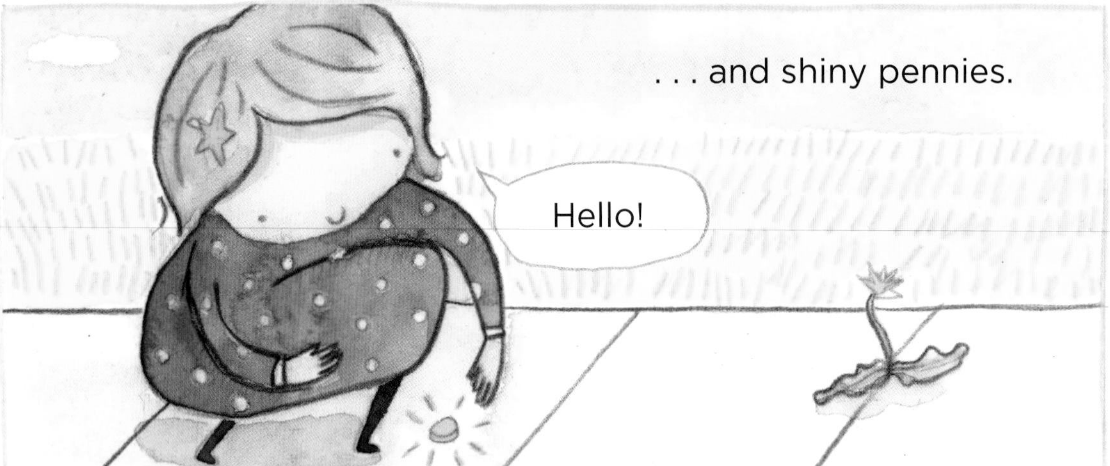
. . . and shiny pennies.
Hello!

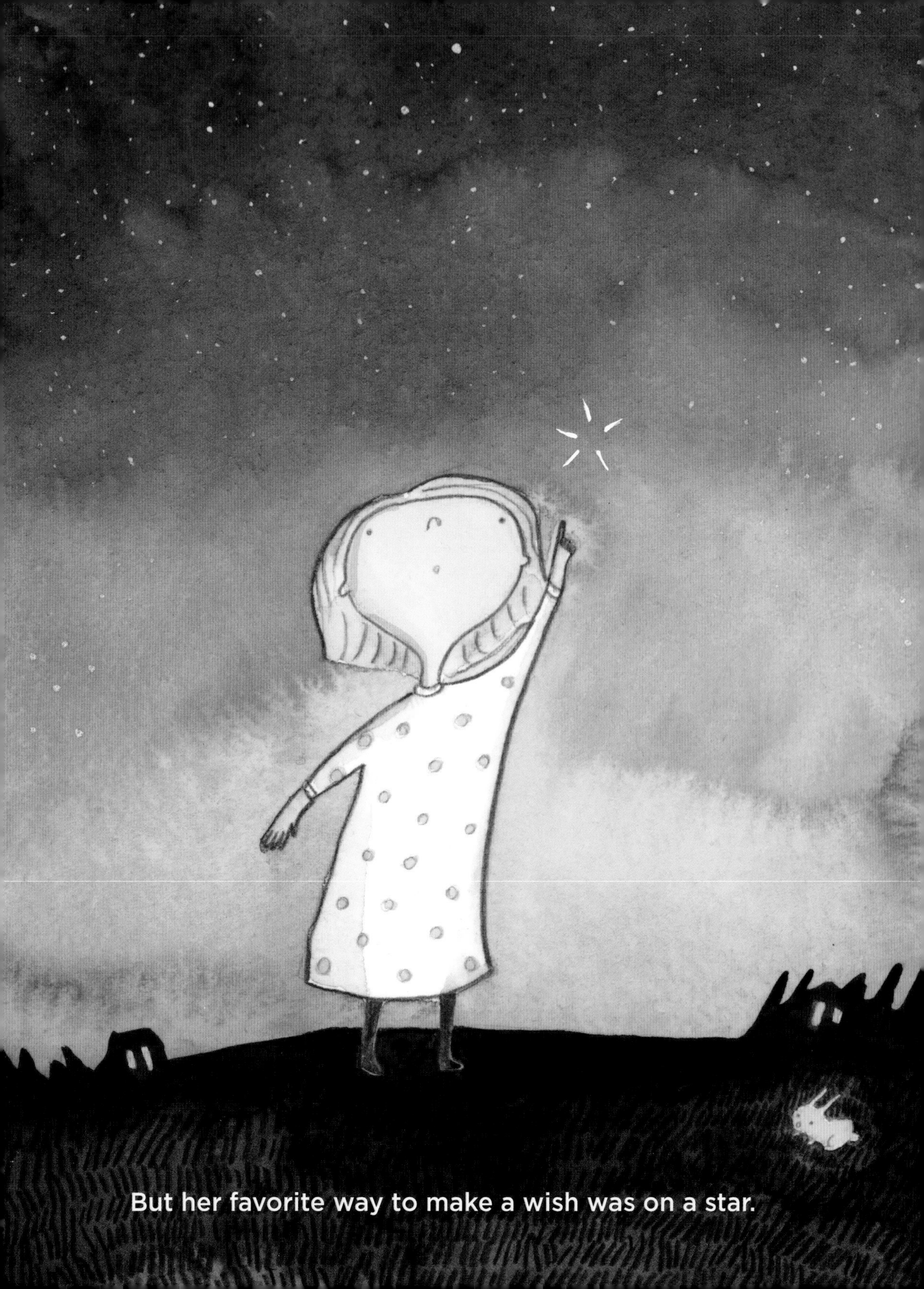

But her favorite way to make a wish was on a star.

But not just any star.

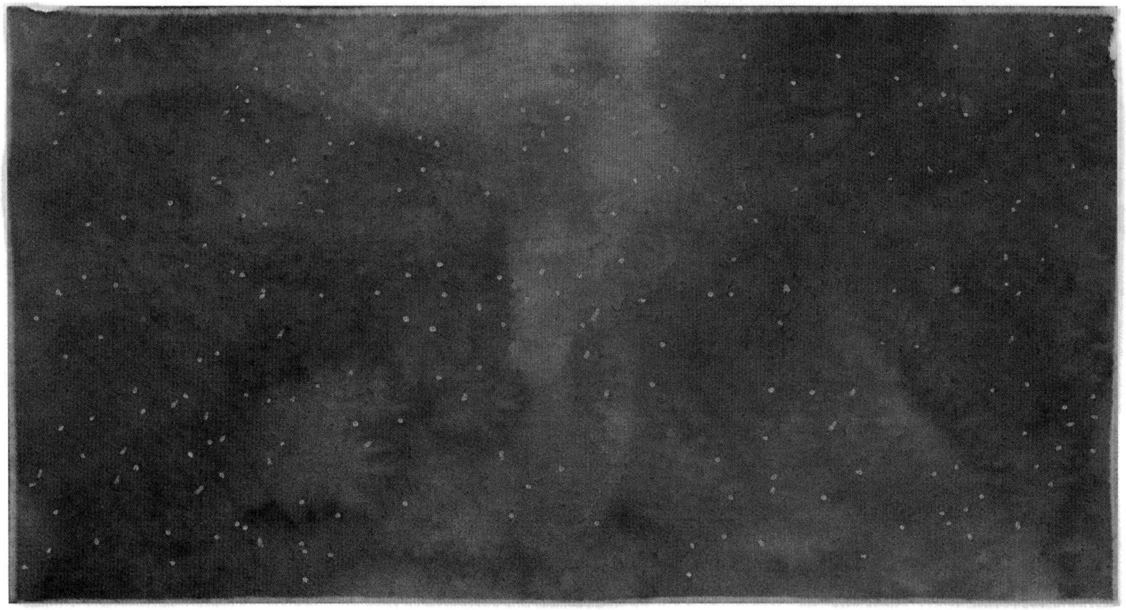

It had to be a falling star.

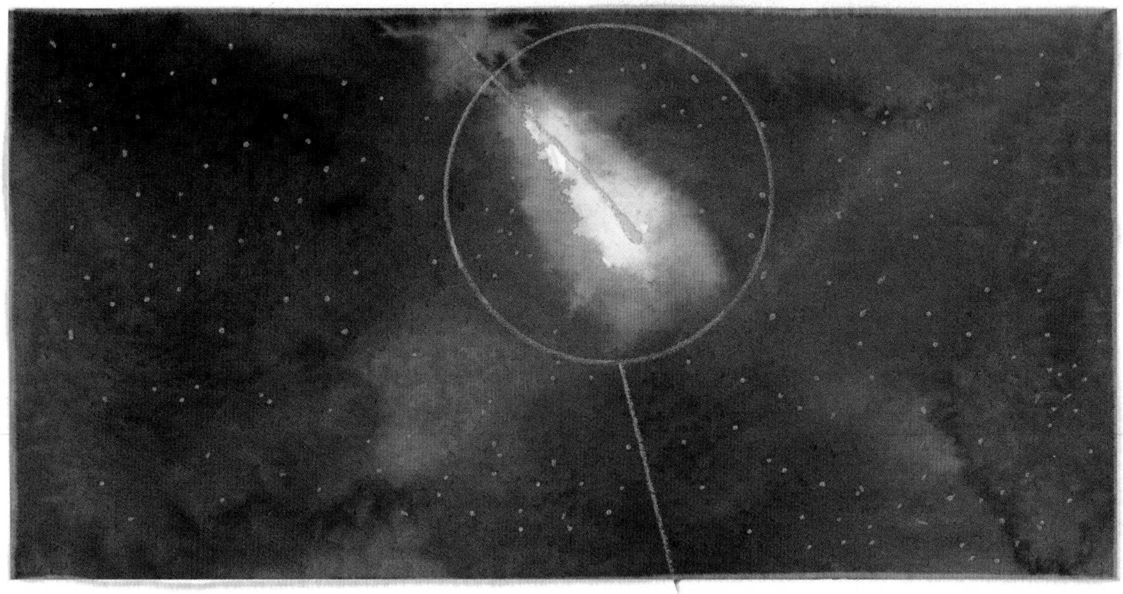

(Quick! Don't miss it!)

One day there was a very special wish that Haylee was ready to make.

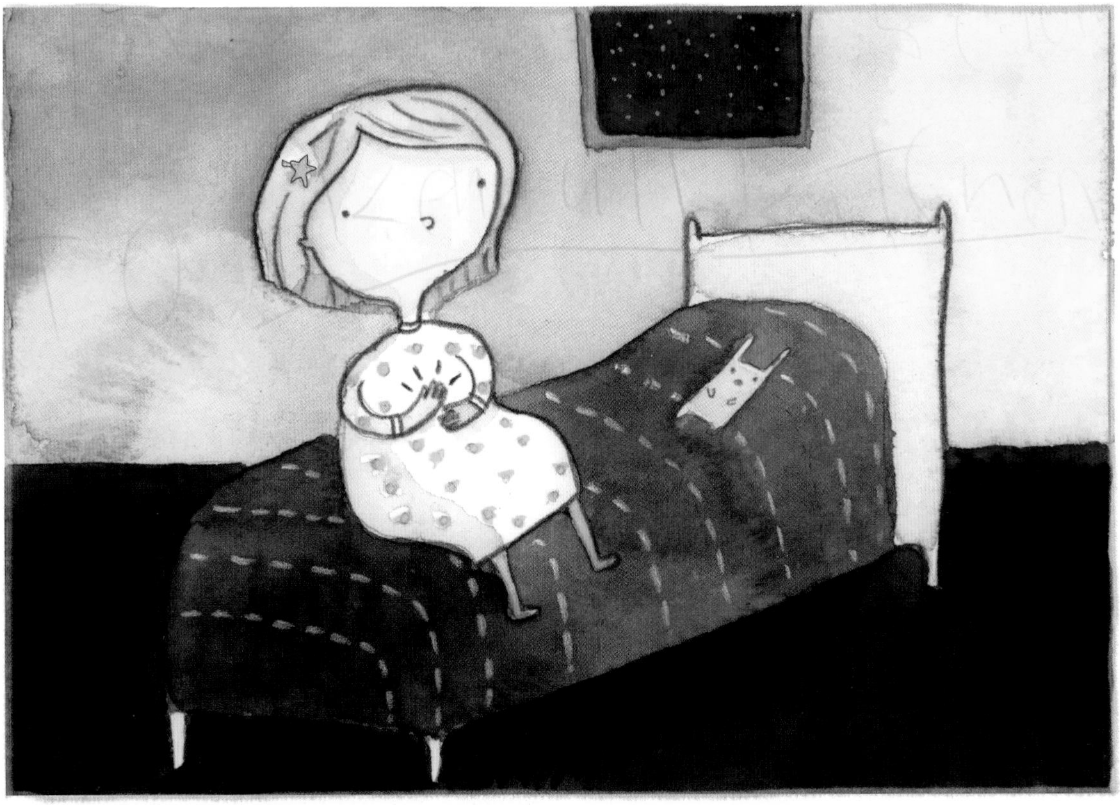

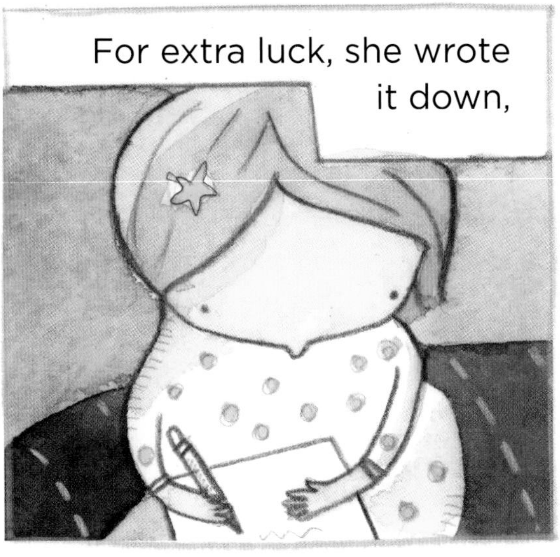
For extra luck, she wrote it down,

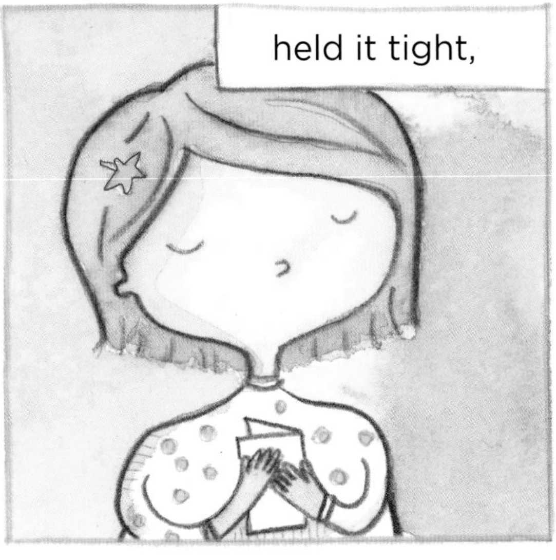
held it tight,

and went outside to look up at the stars.

The sky twinkled.

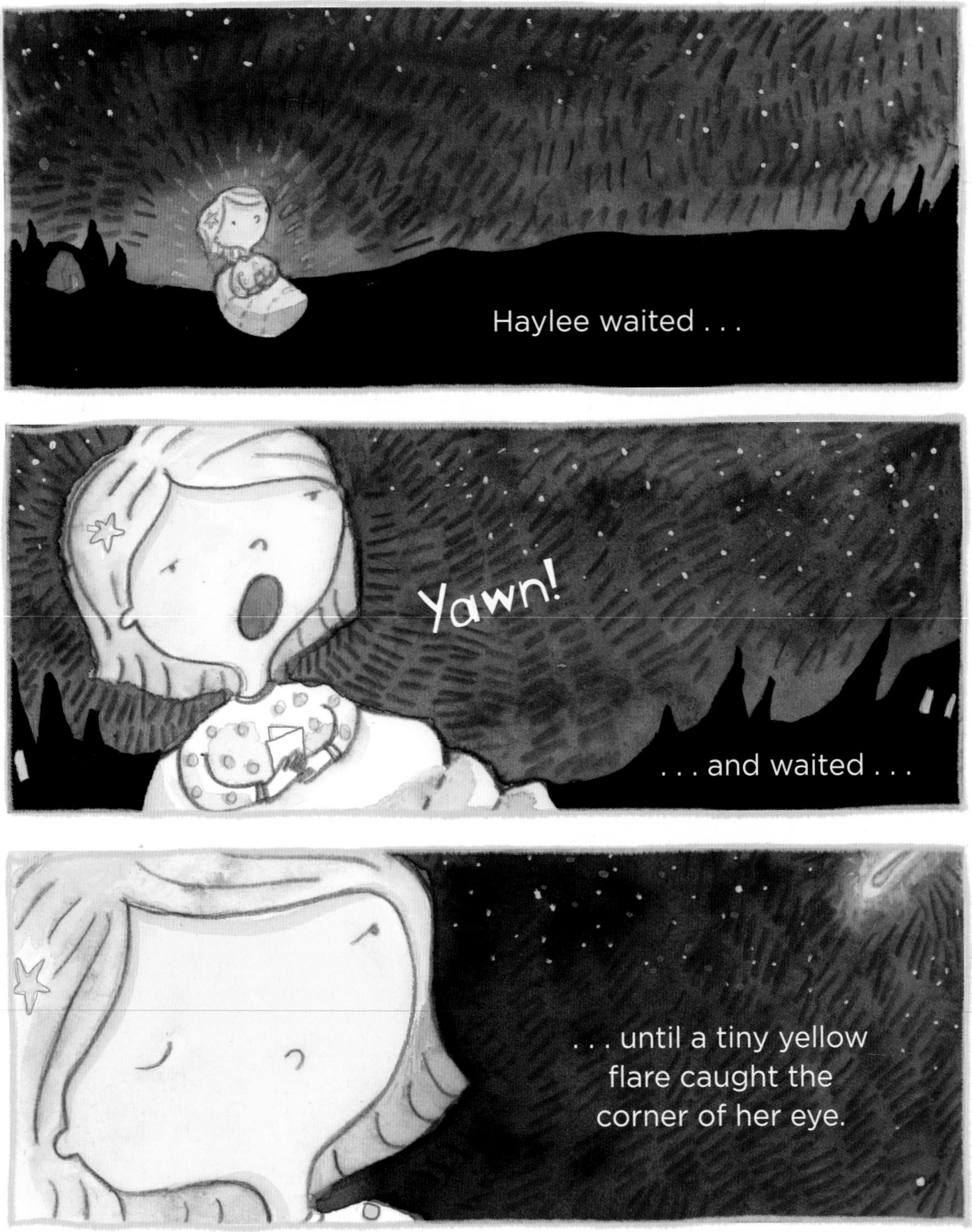
Haylee waited . . .
Yawn!
. . . and waited . . .
. . . until a tiny yellow flare caught the corner of her eye.

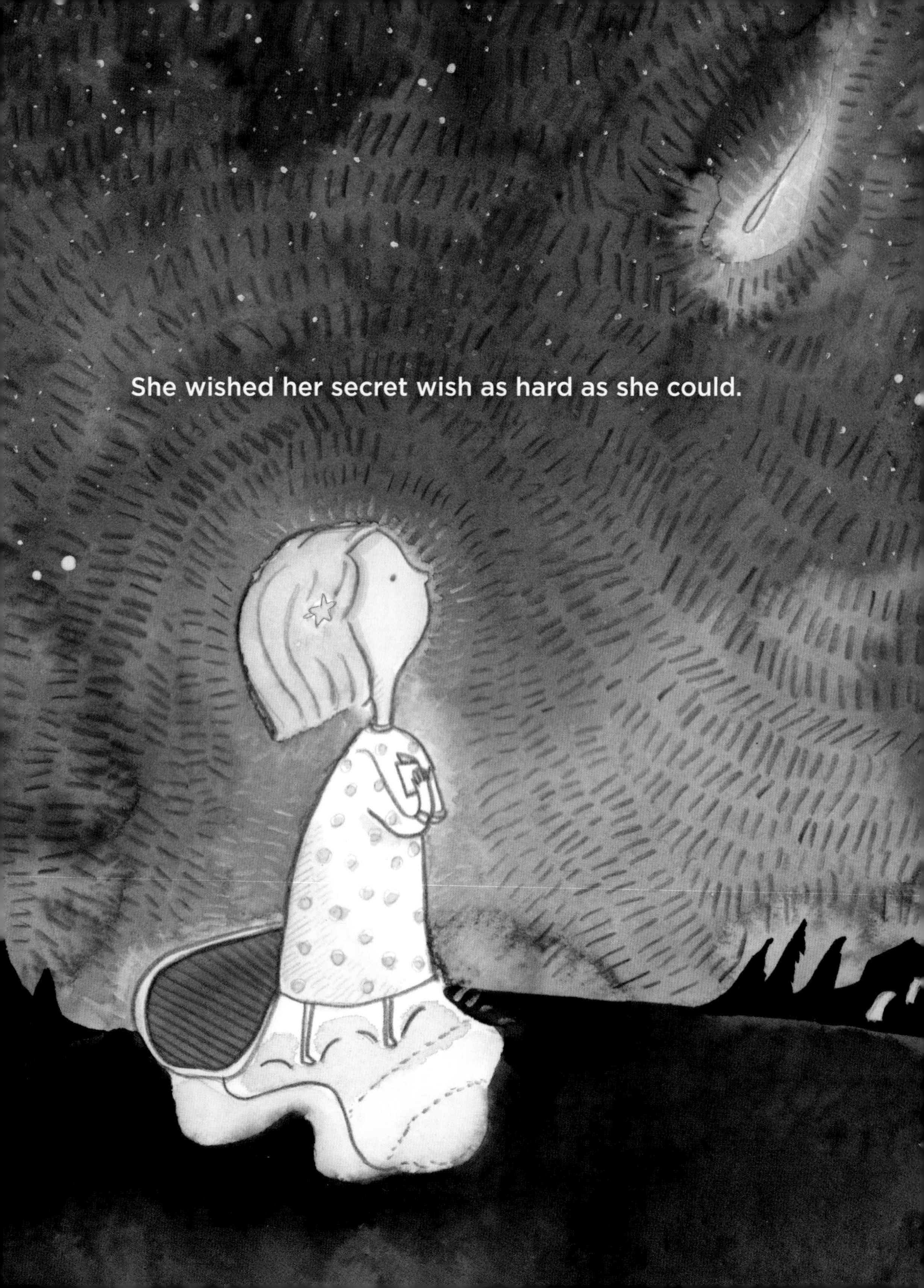

She wished her secret wish as hard as she could.

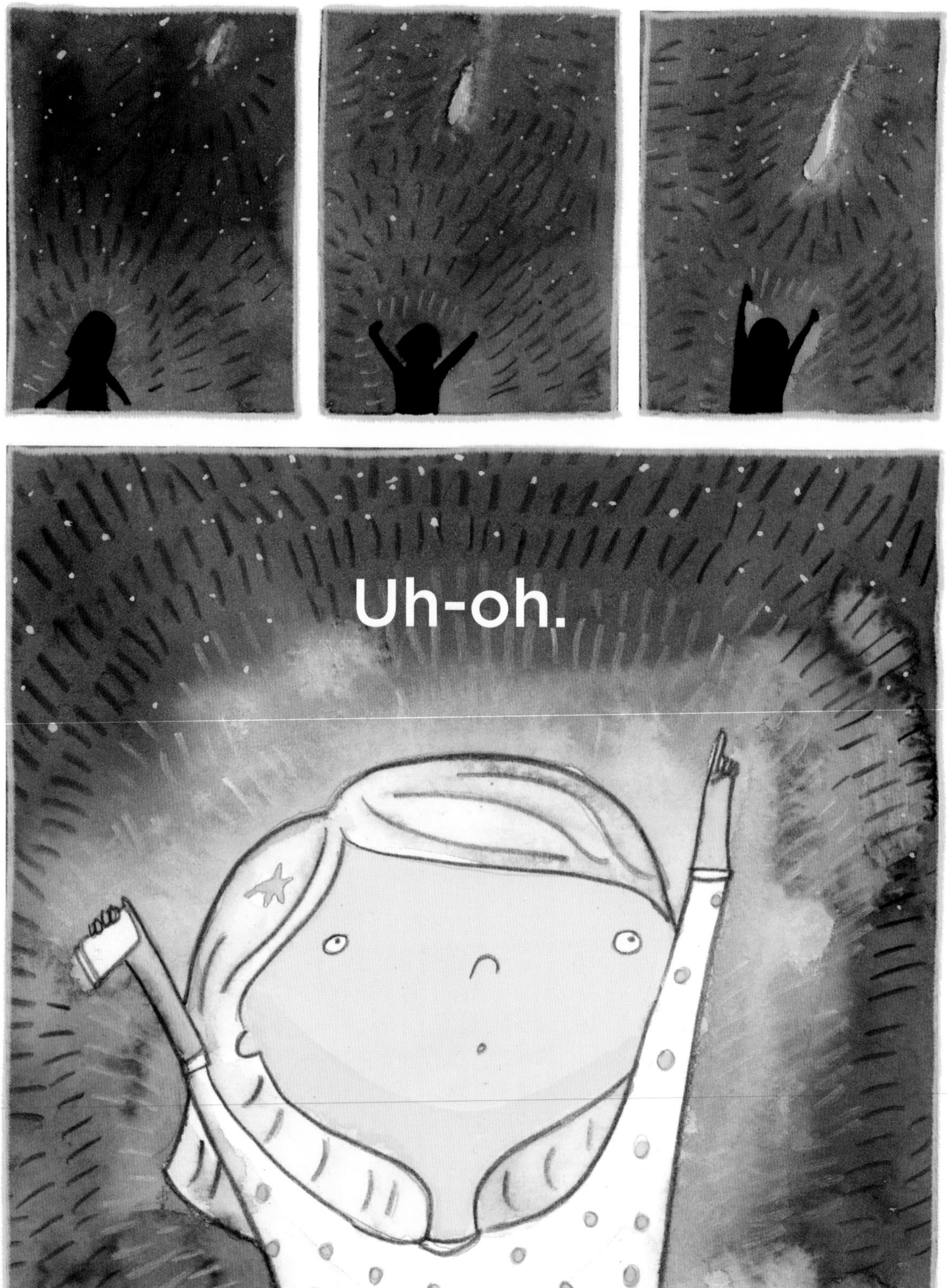
Uh-oh.

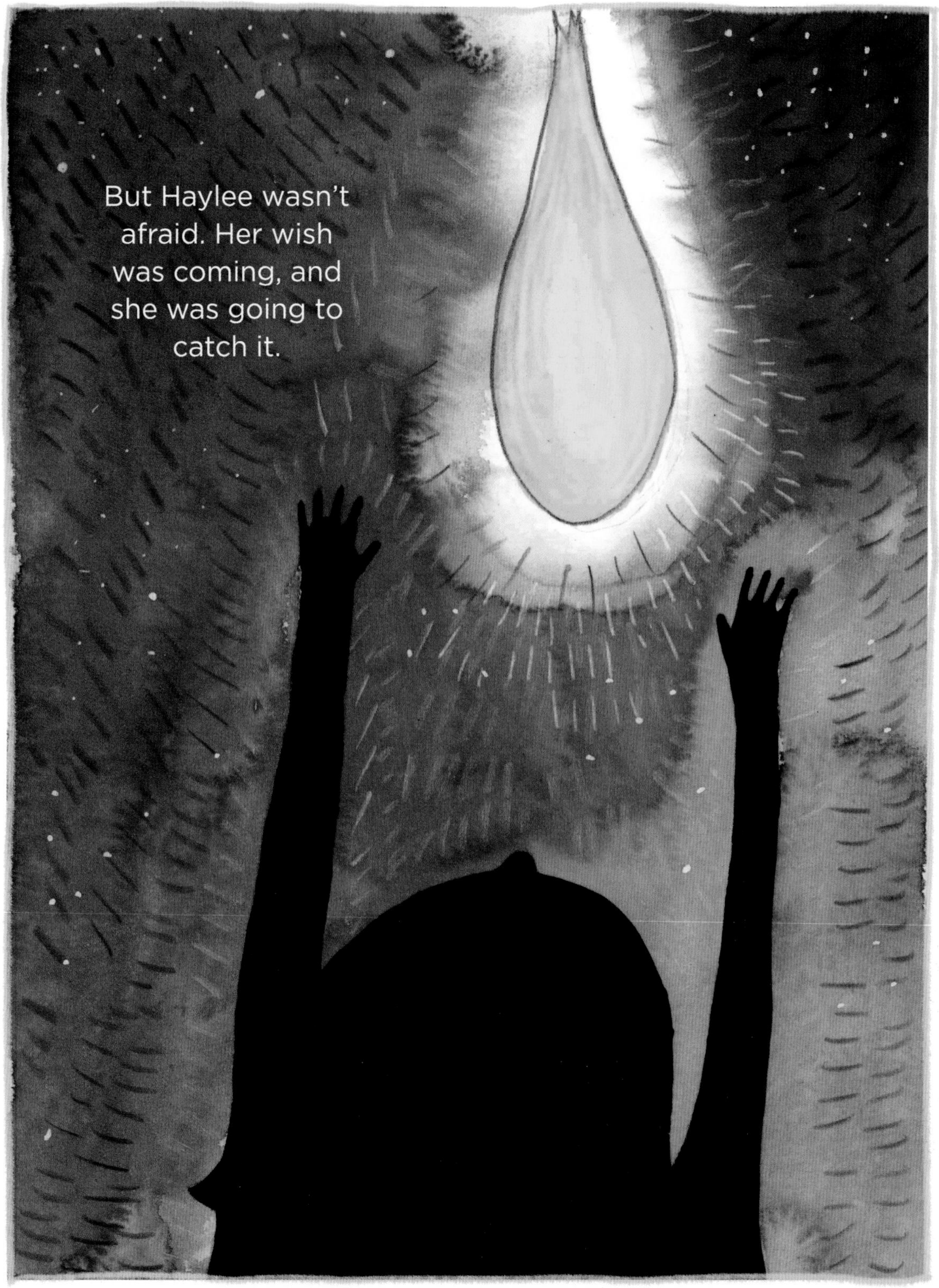
But Haylee wasn't
afraid. Her wish
was coming, and
she was going to
catch it.

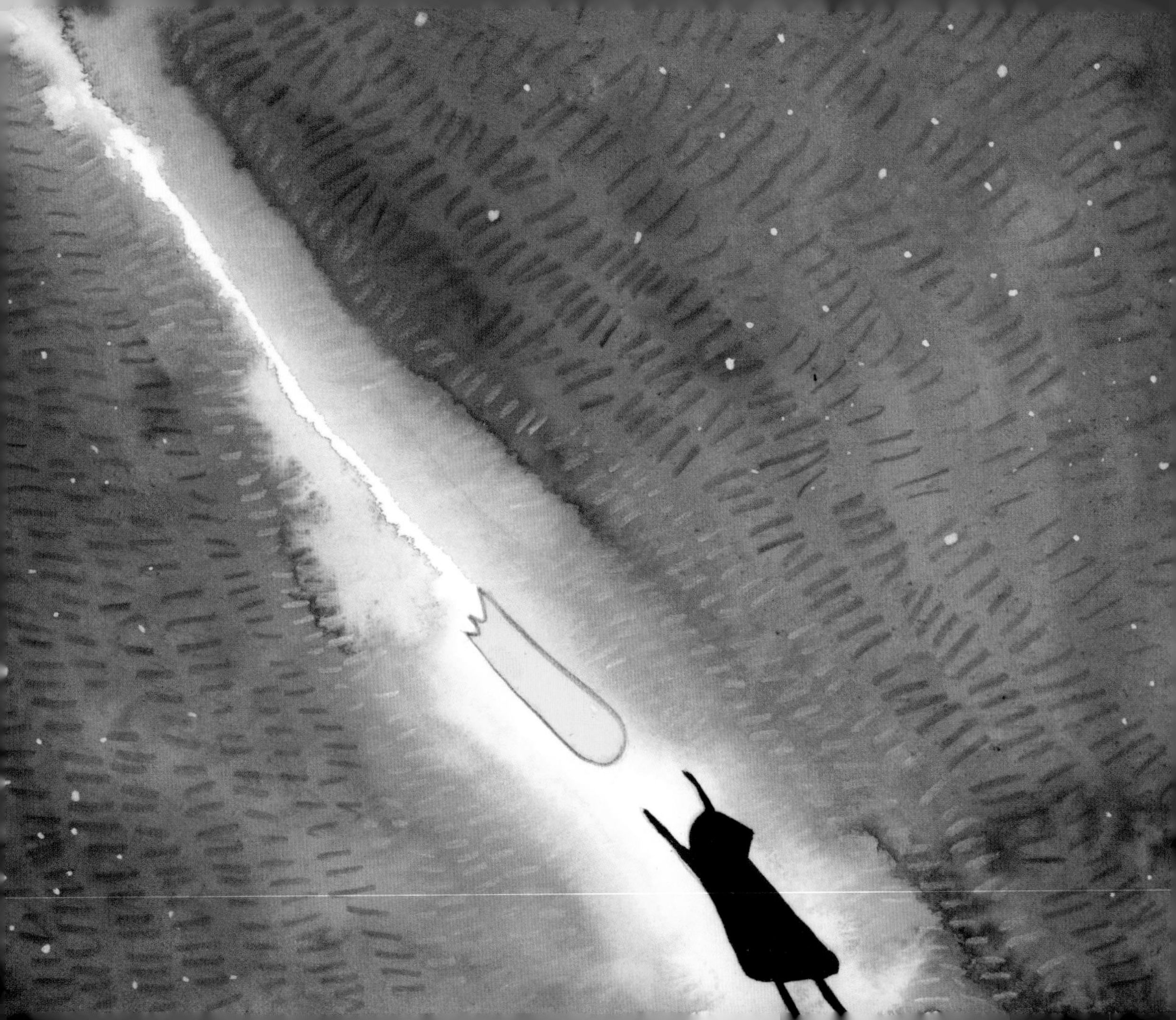

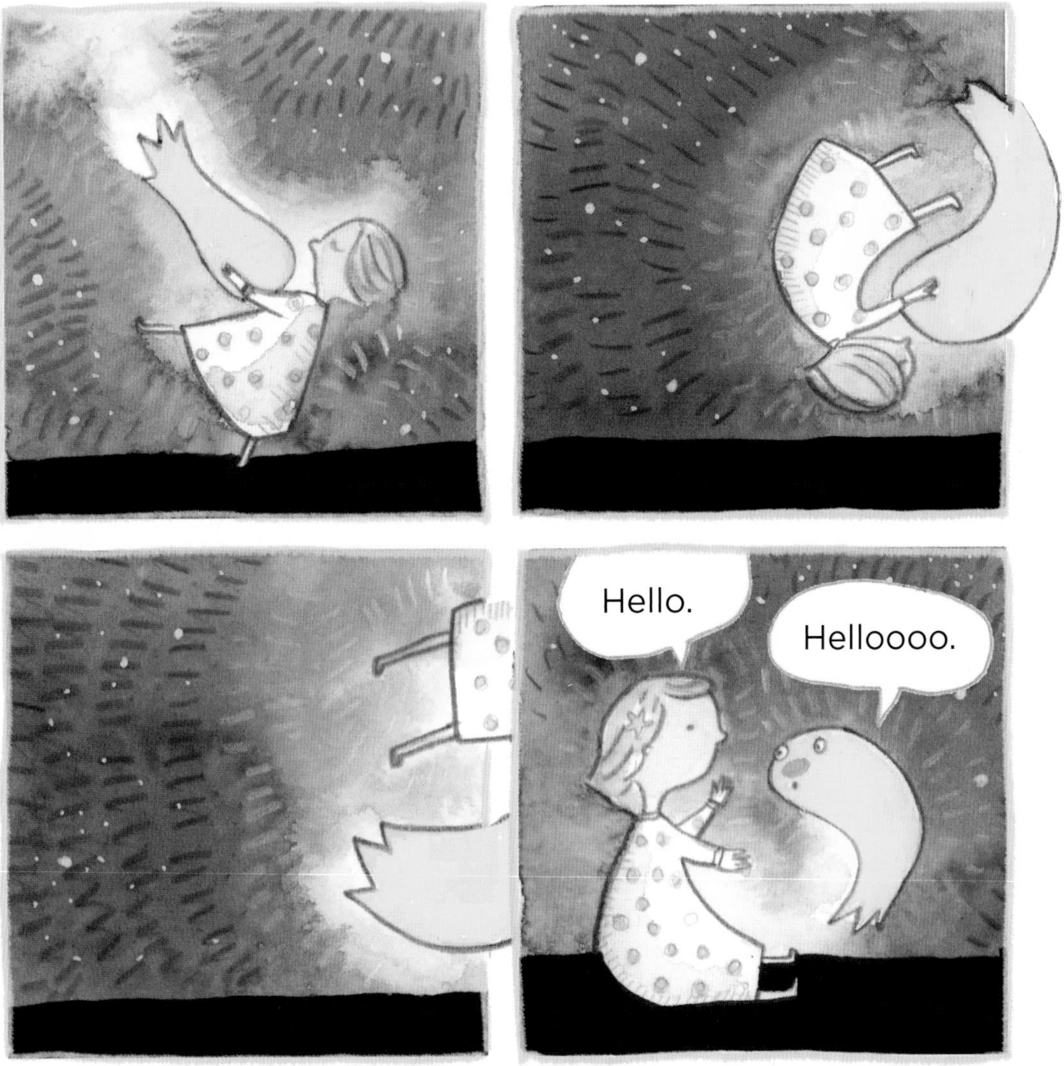
Hello.
Helloooo.

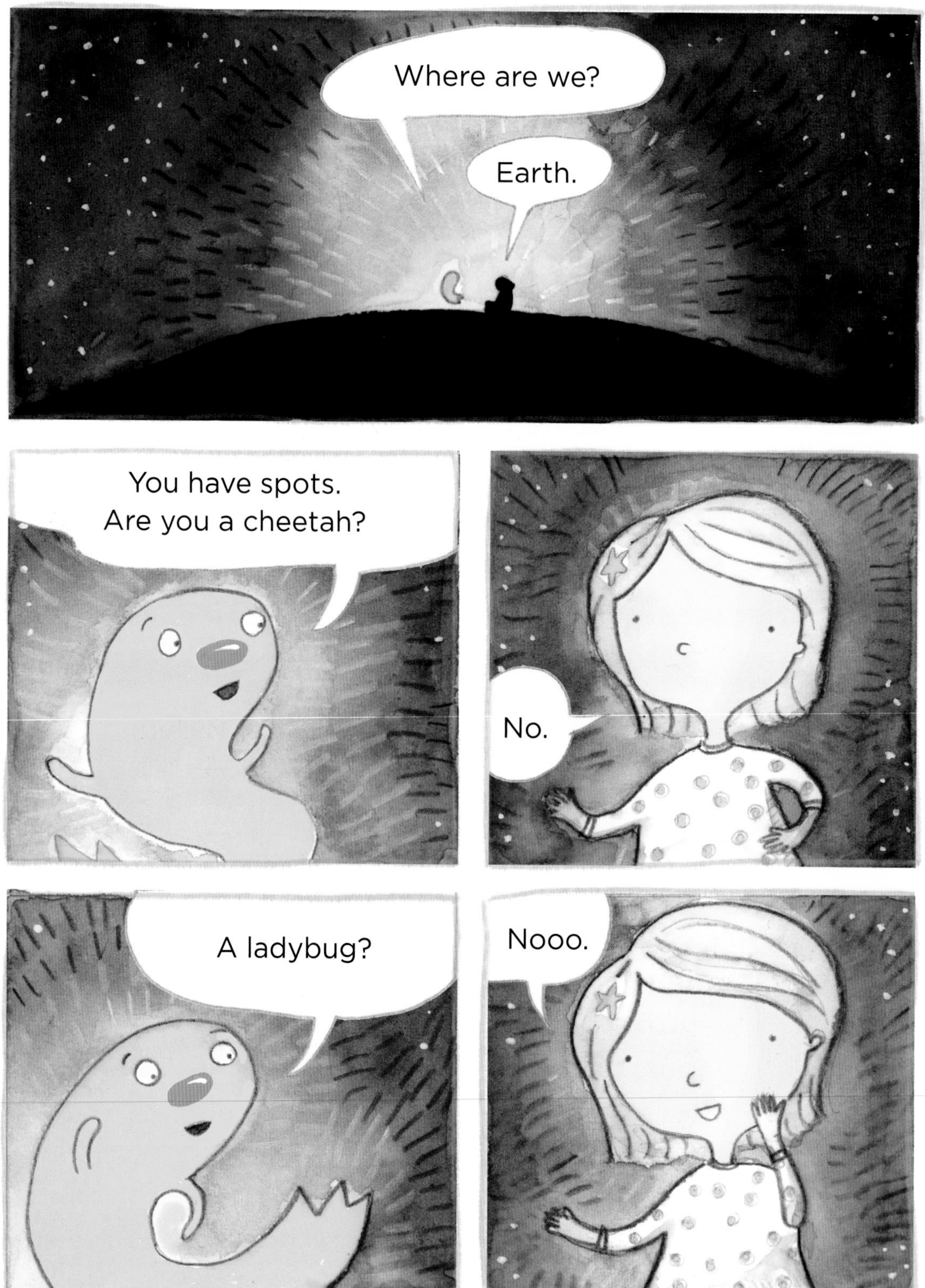
Where are we?
Earth.
You have spots. Are you a cheetah?
No.
A ladybug?
Nooo.

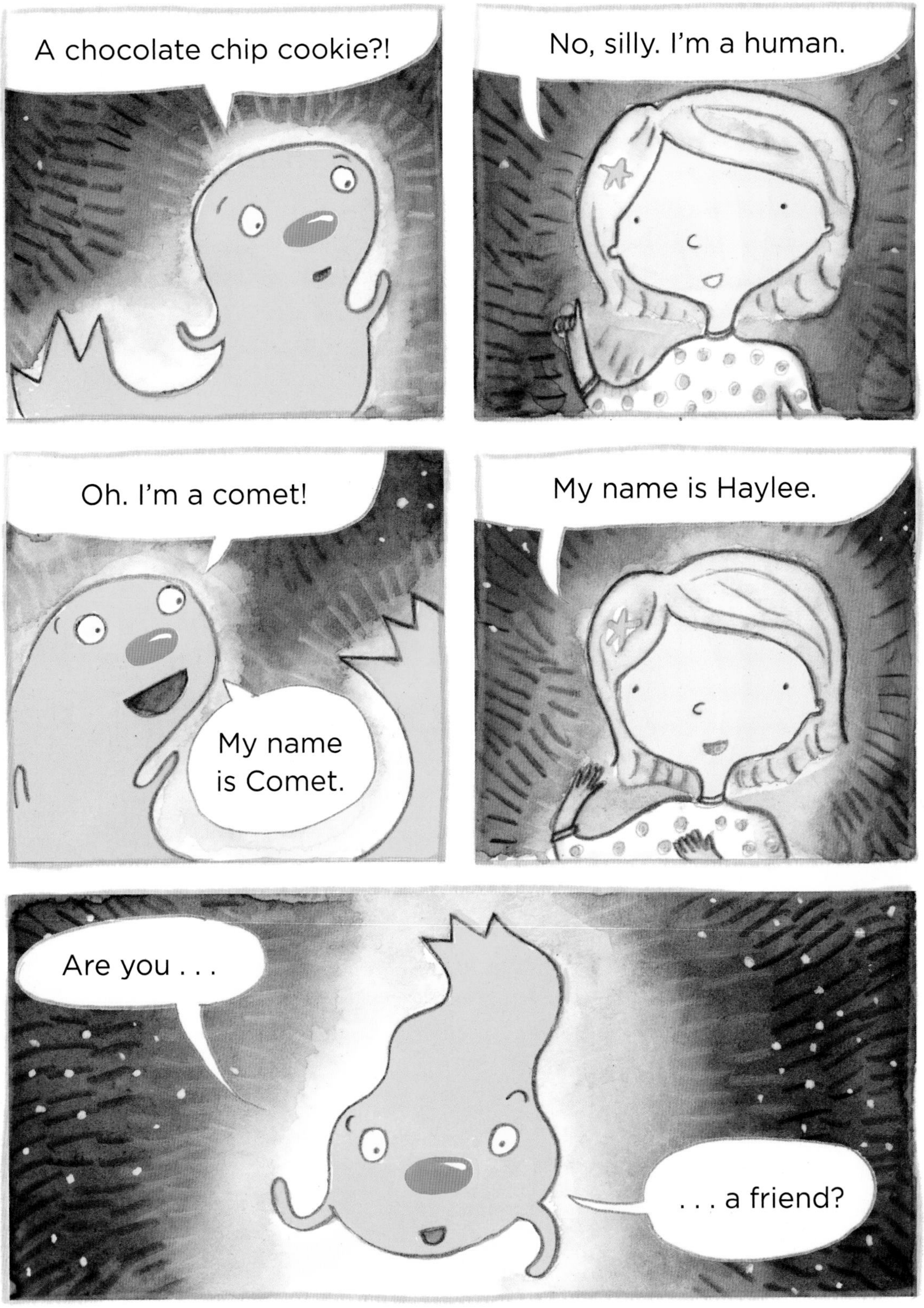
A chocolate chip cookie?!
No, silly. I'm a human.
Oh. I'm a comet!
My name is Comet.
My name is Haylee.
Are you . . .
. . . a friend?

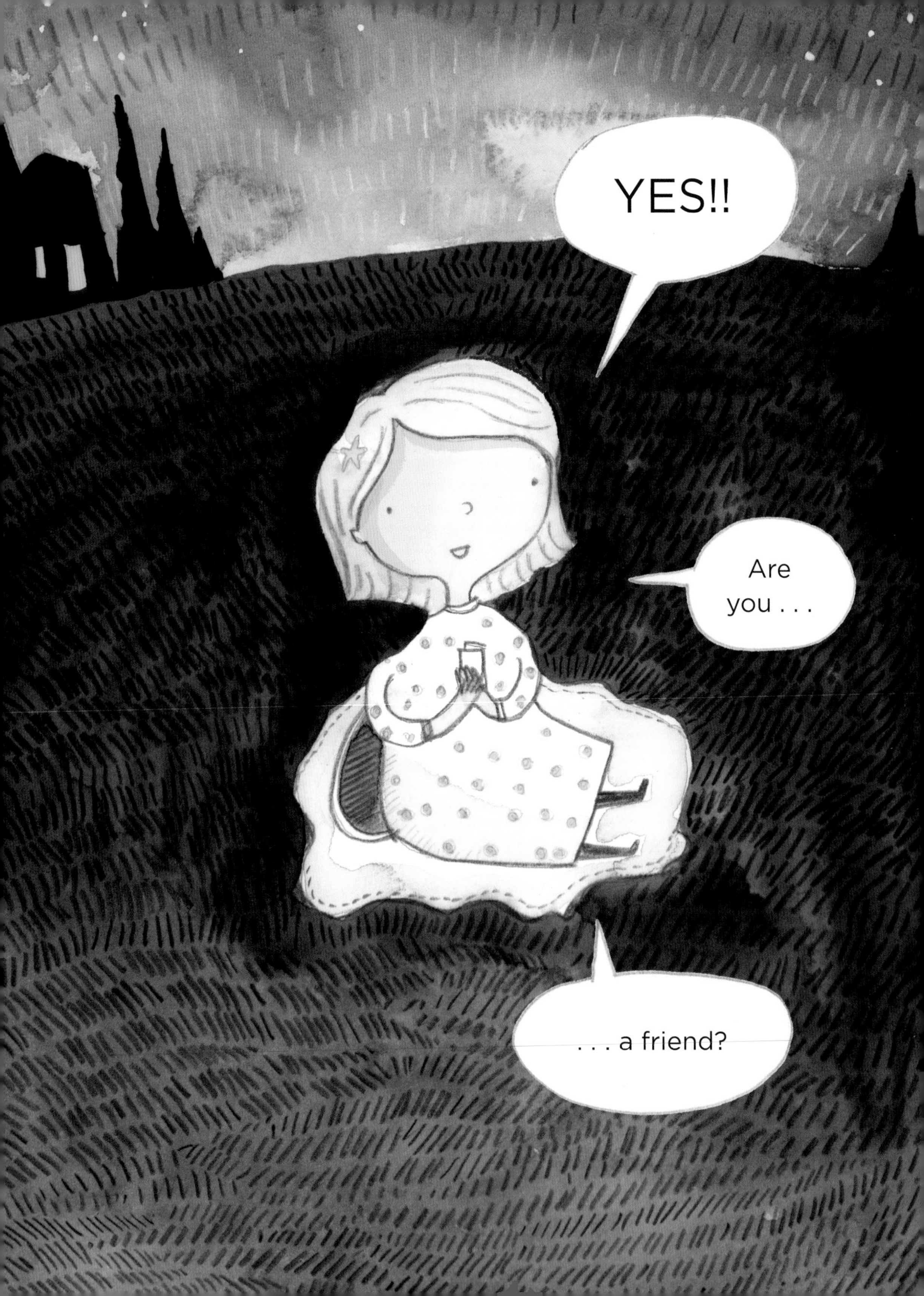
YES!!
Are you . . .
. . . a friend?

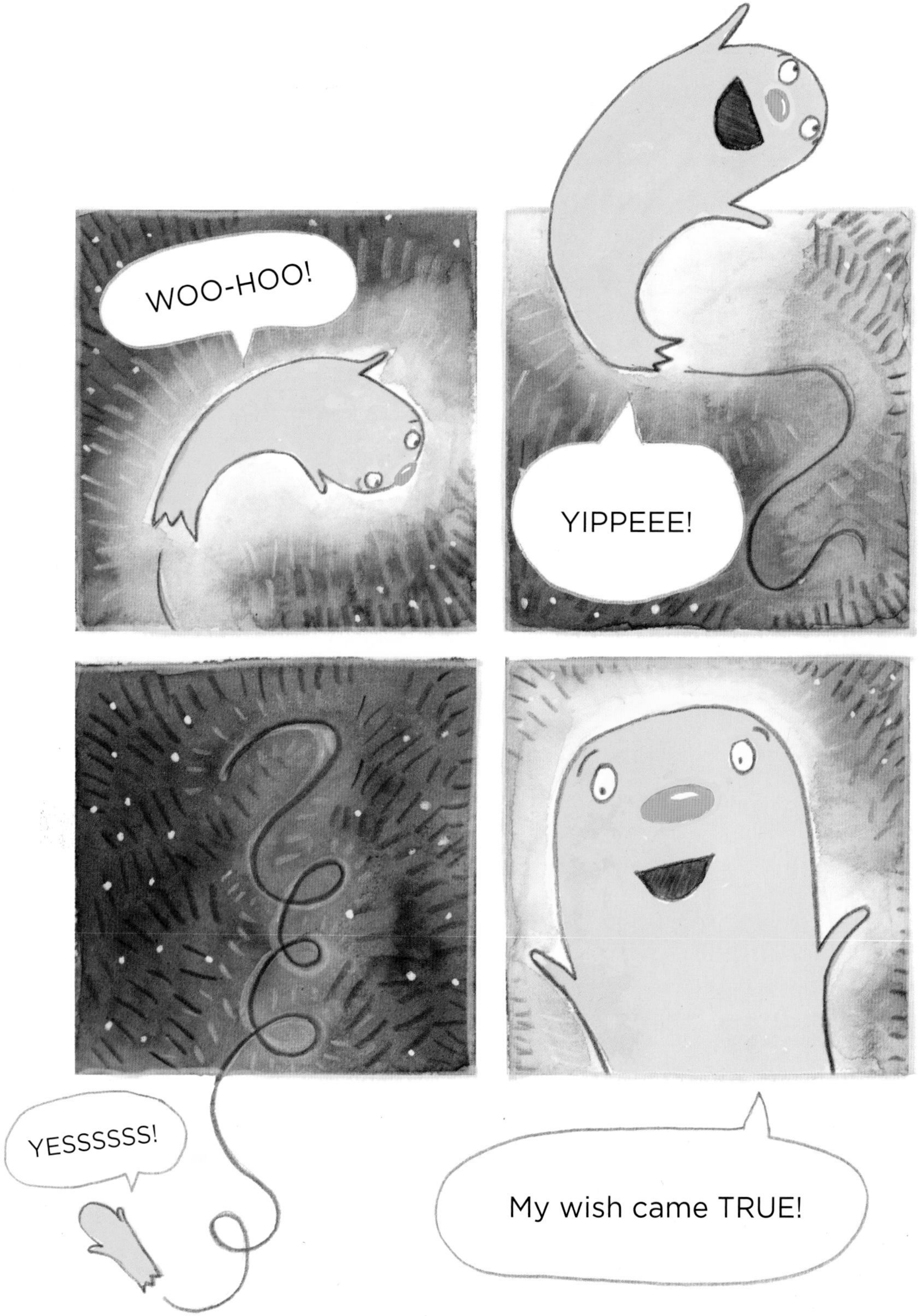
WOO-HOO!
YIPPEEE!
YESSSSSS!
My wish came TRUE!

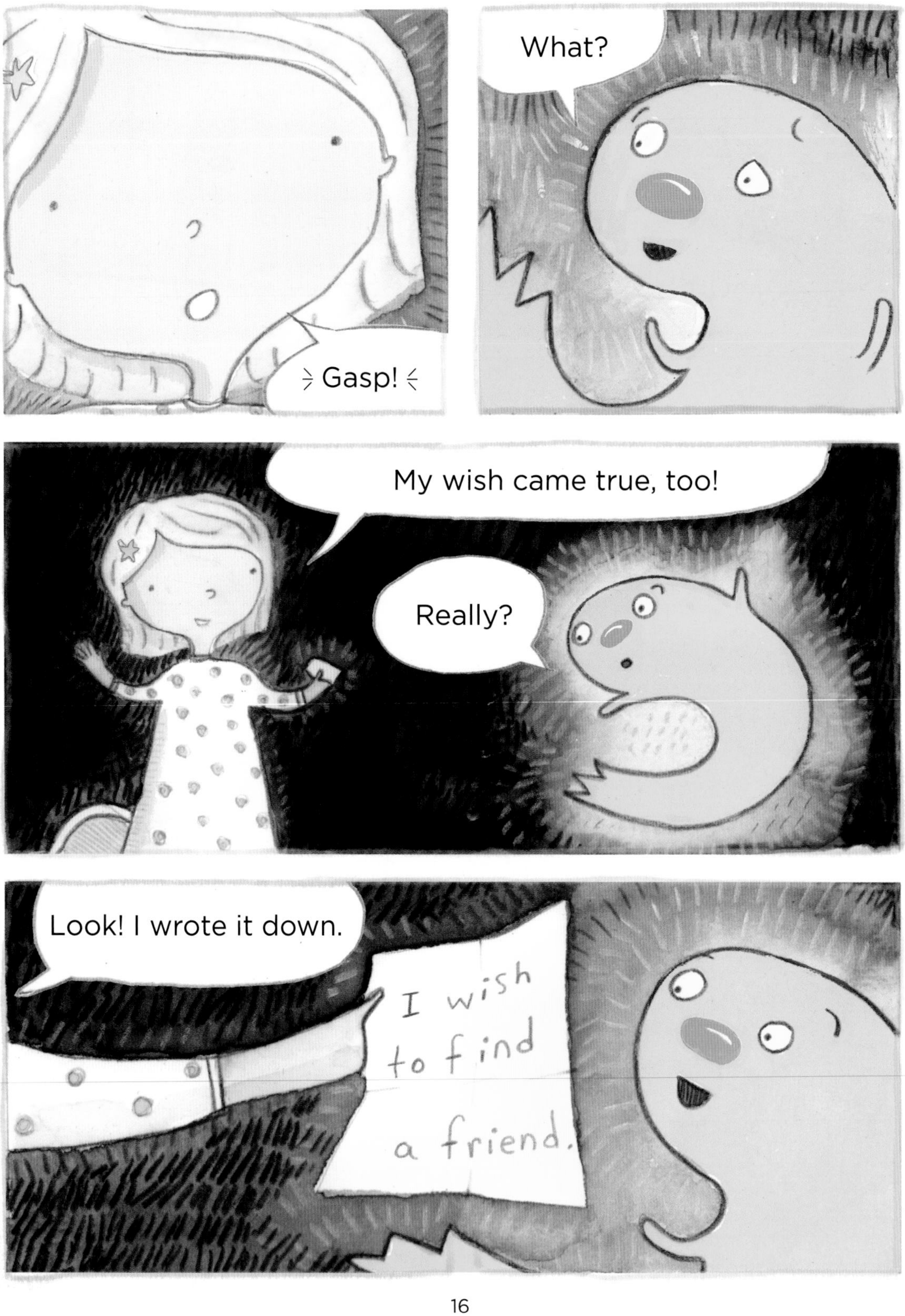
Gasp!
What?
My wish came true, too!
Really?
Look! I wrote it down.
I wish to find a friend.

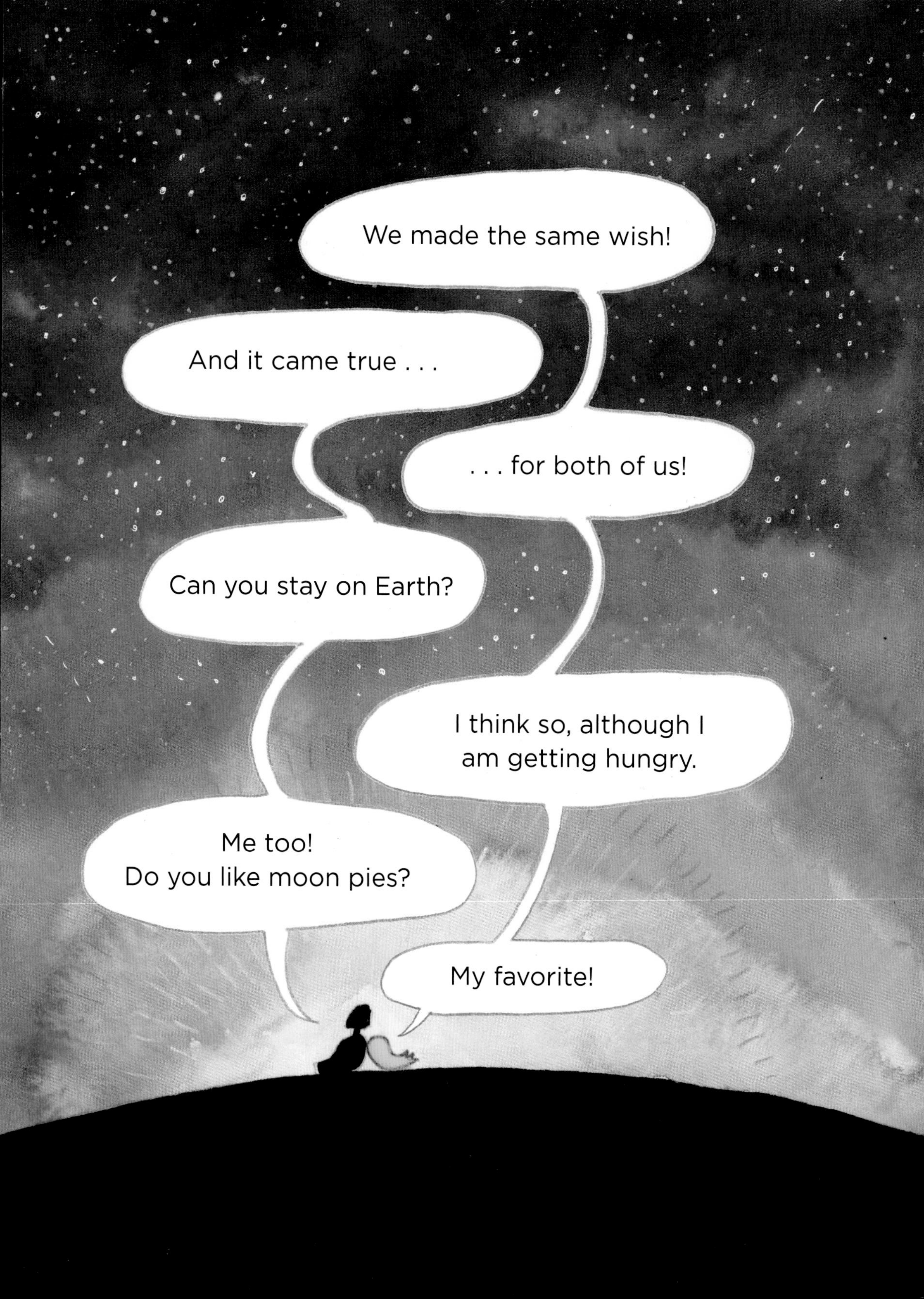
We made the same wish!
And it came true . . .
. . . for both of us!
Can you stay on Earth?
I think so, although I am getting hungry.
Me too! Do you like moon pies?
My favorite!

Other things to make wishes on:

Paper Lanterns

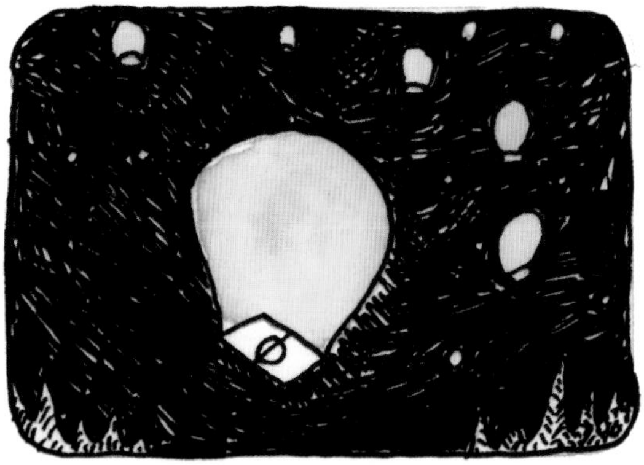

Birthday Candles

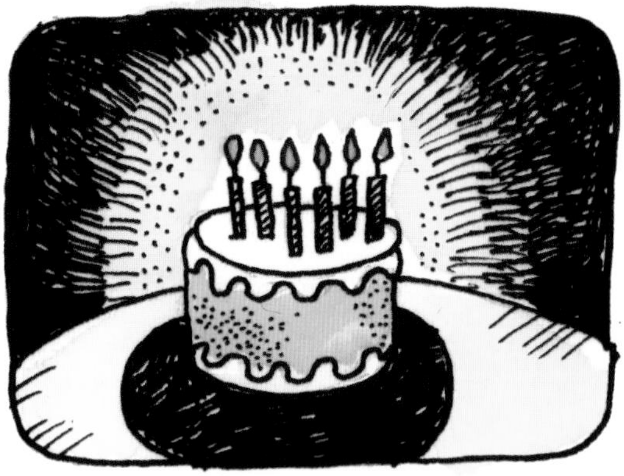

Rainbows

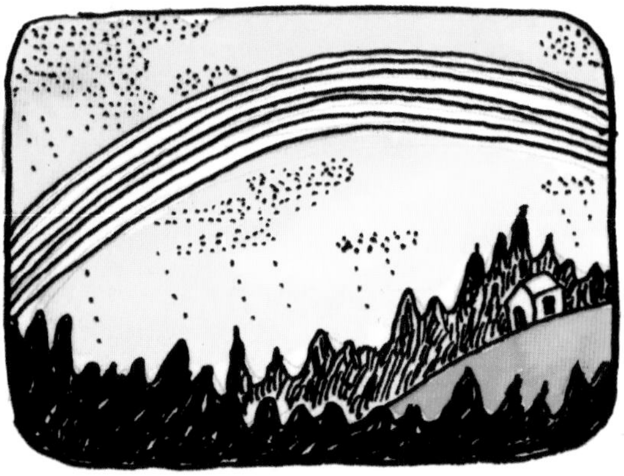

Eyelashes

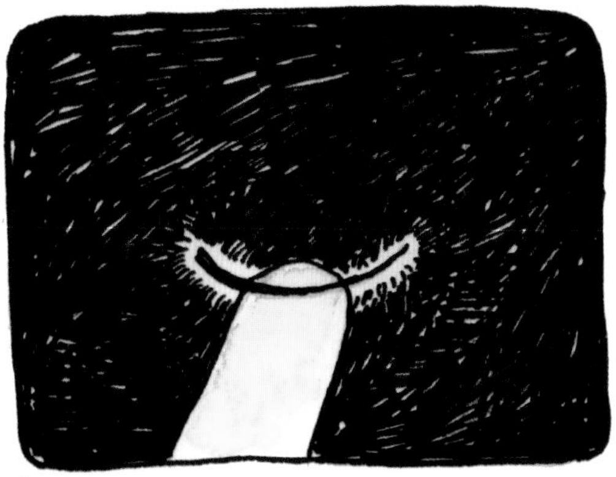

Feathers

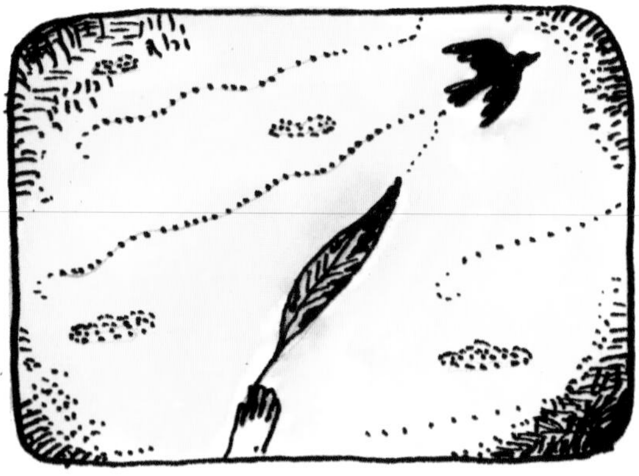

Ladybugs

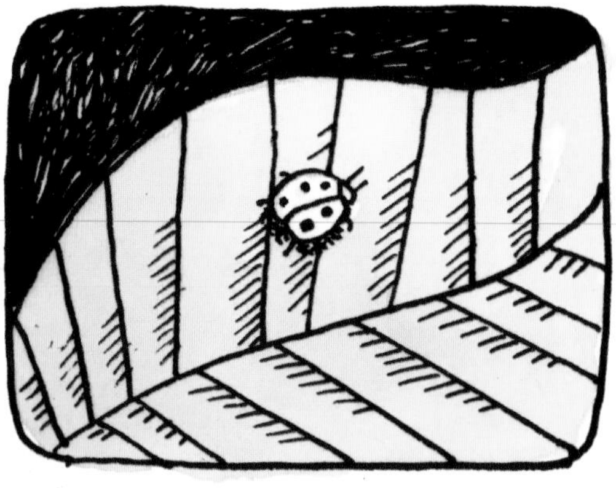

FRIEND SHIP

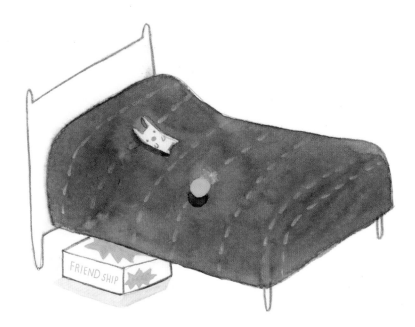

THE FRIEND SHIP

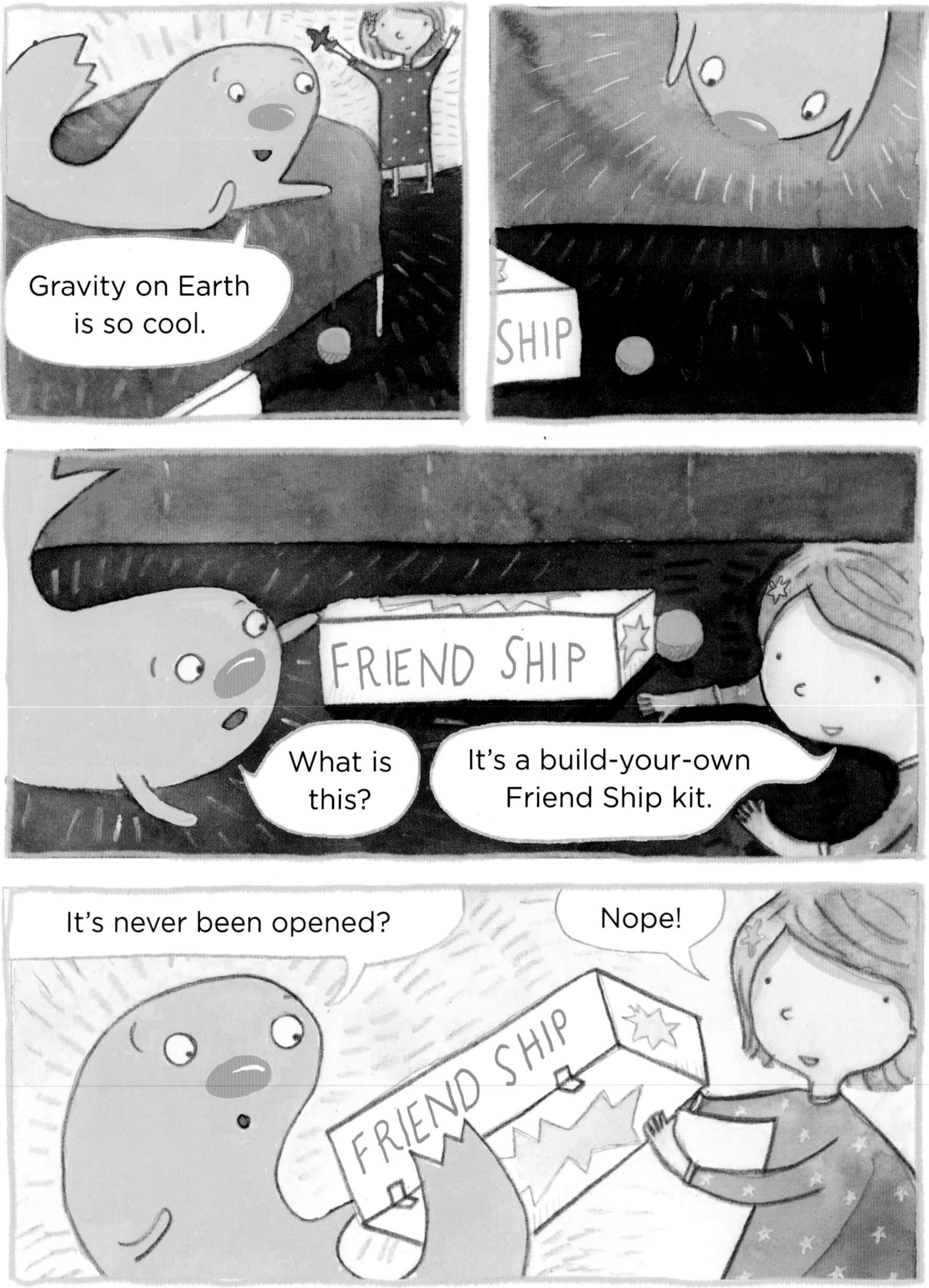
Gravity on Earth is so cool.
SHIP
FRIEND SHIP
What is this?
It's a build-your-own Friend Ship kit.
It's never been opened?
Nope!
FRIEND SHIP

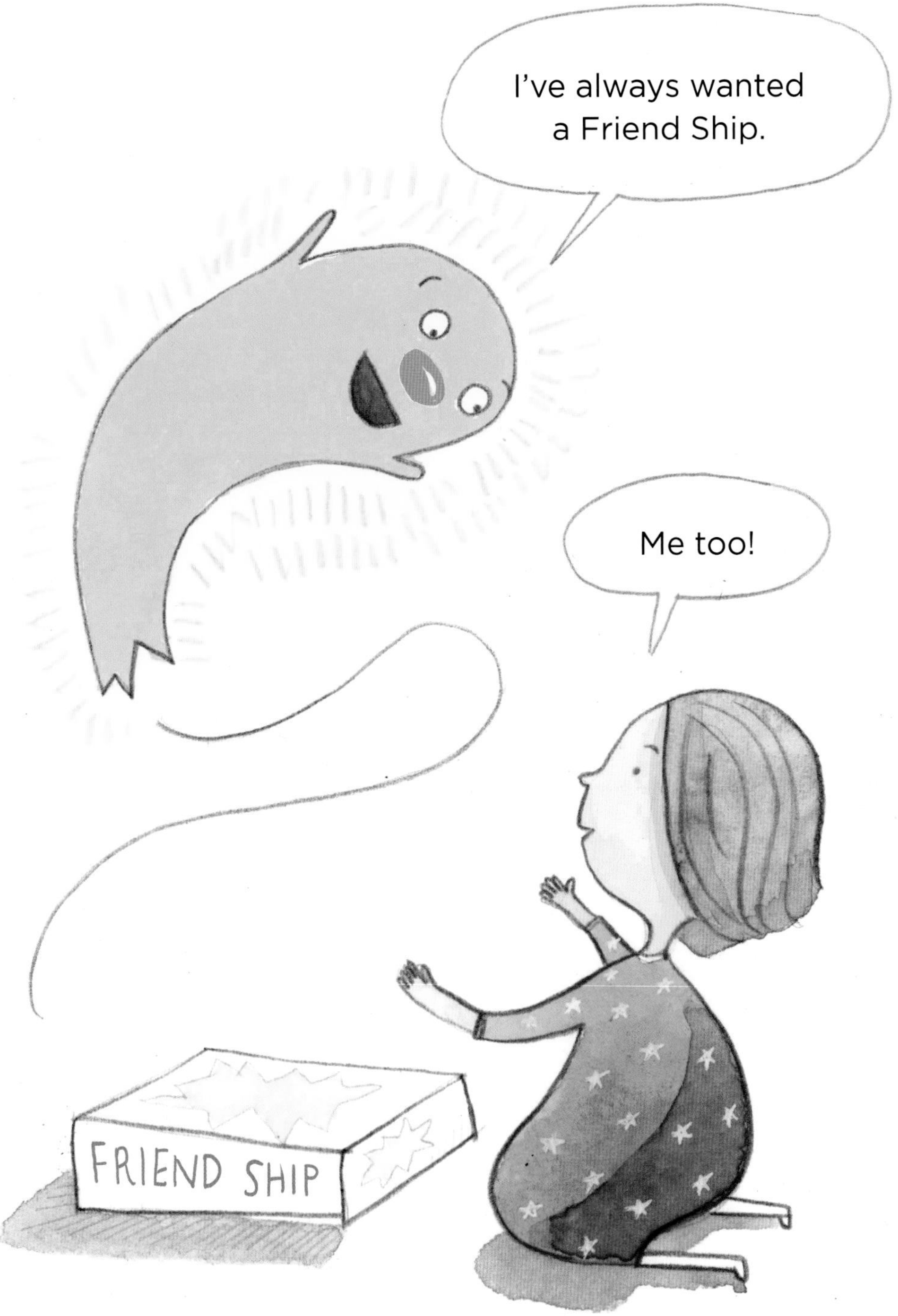
I've always wanted
a Friend Ship.
Me too!
FRIEND SHIP

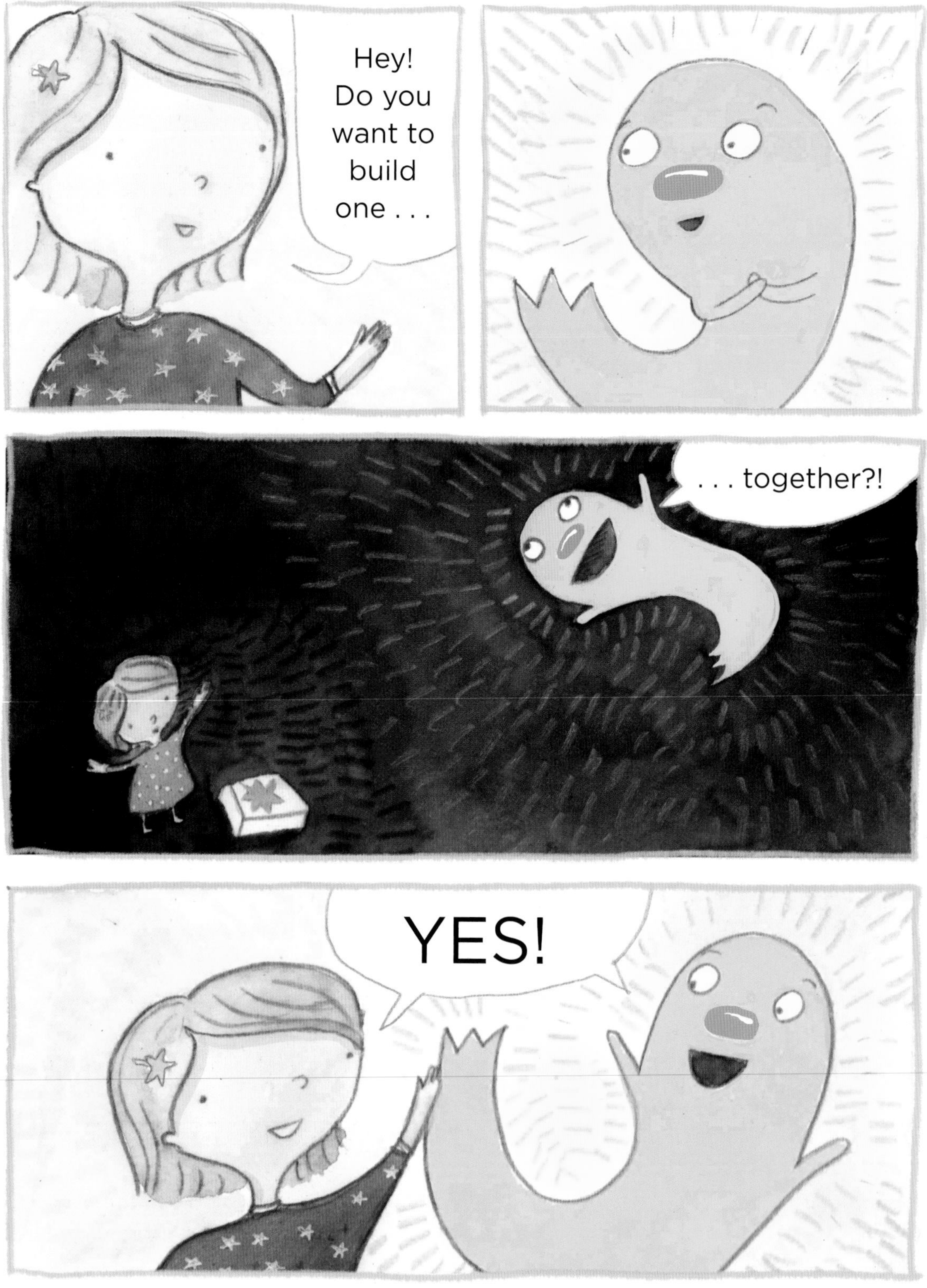
Hey! Do you want to build one . . .
. . . together?!
YES!

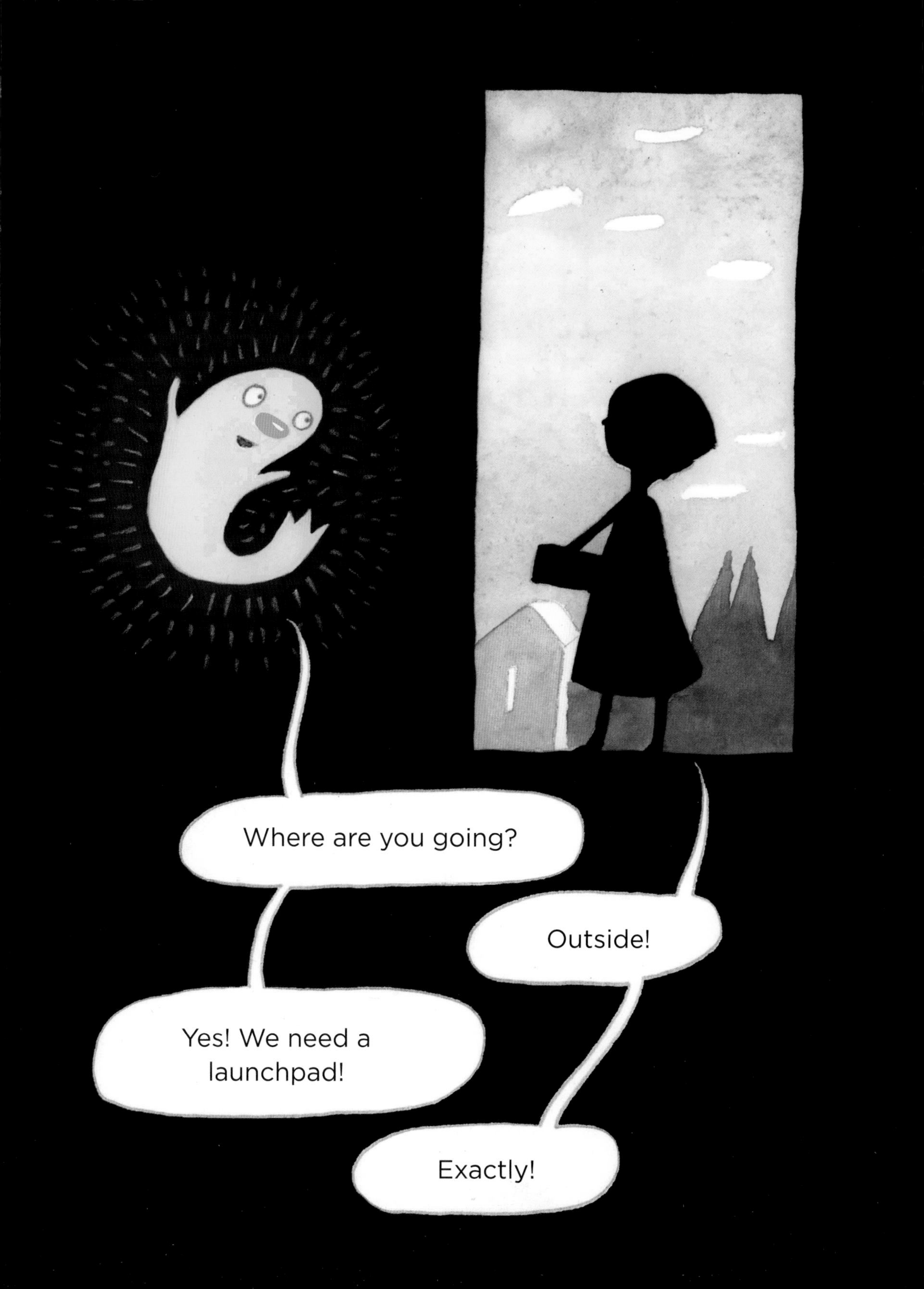
Where are you going?
Outside!
Yes! We need a launchpad!
Exactly!

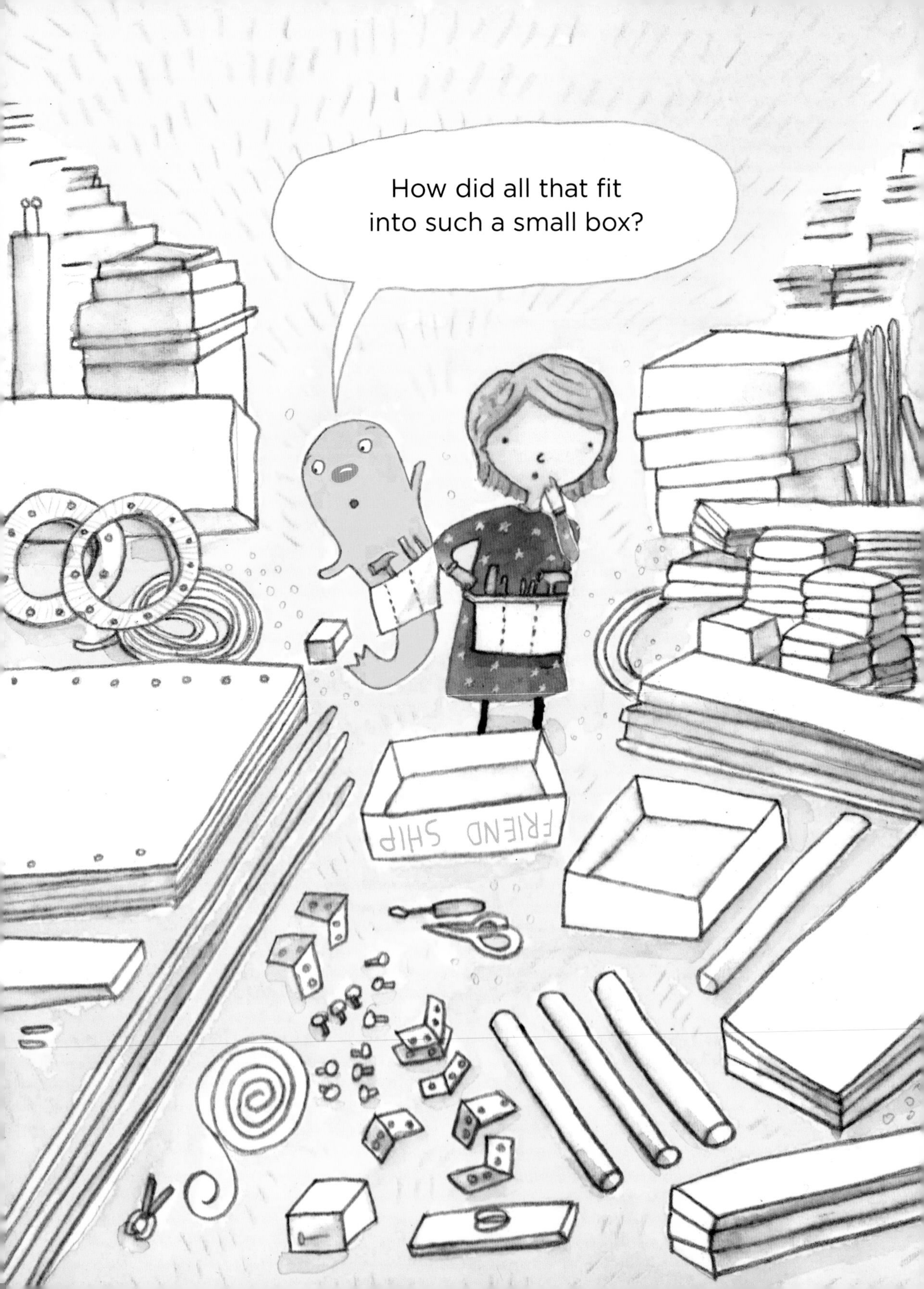
How did all that fit
into such a small box?
FRIEND SHIP

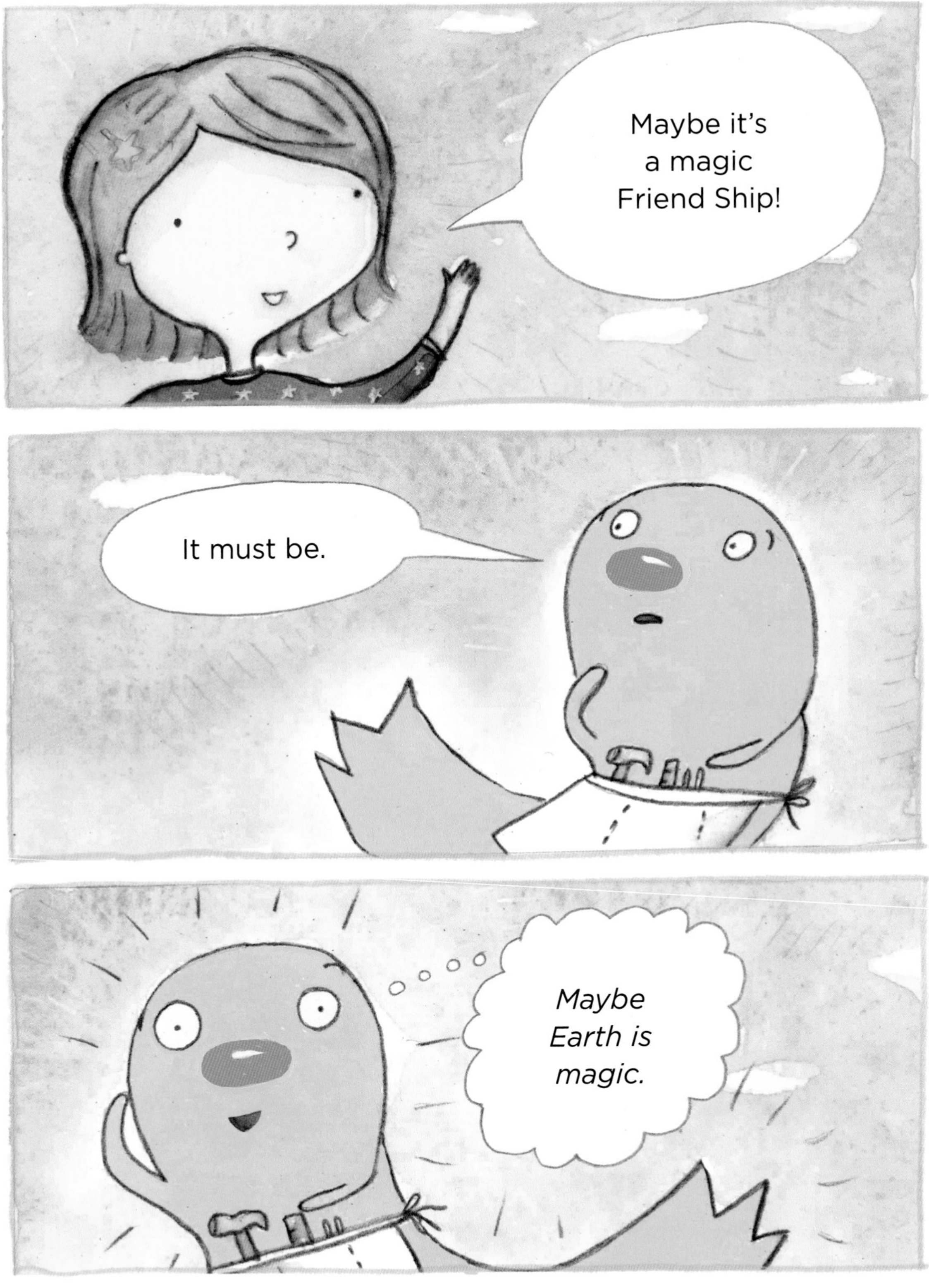
Maybe it's a magic Friend Ship!
It must be.
Maybe Earth is magic.

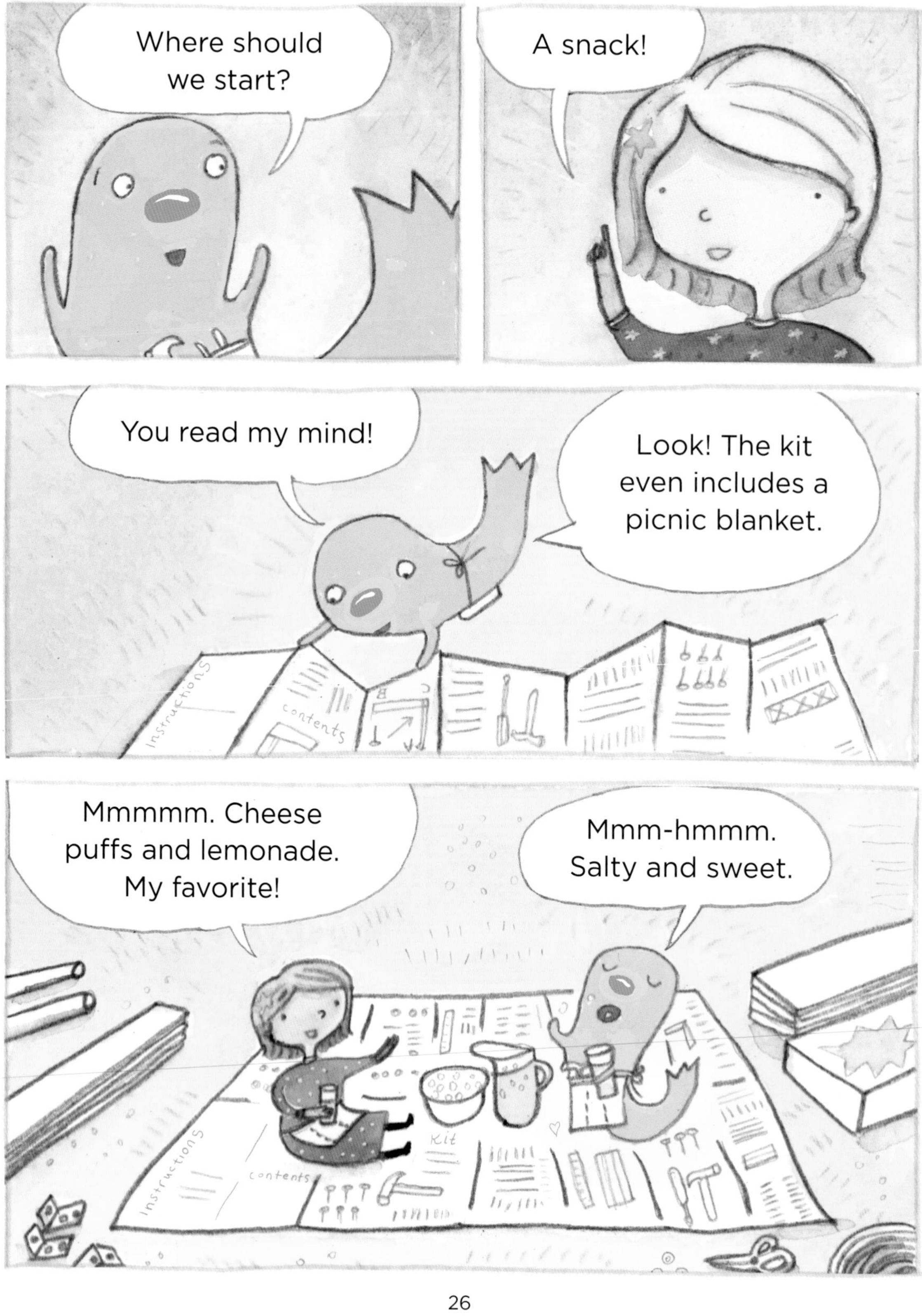
Where should we start?
A snack!
You read my mind!
Look! The kit even includes a picnic blanket.
Mmmmm. Cheese puffs and lemonade. My favorite!
Mmm-hmmm. Salty and sweet.

There are a lot of parts here.
Do you see any instructions?
No.
We'll just have to piece it together as best we can.
That's okay! I can see it clearly in my imagination.
Me too! If I start on the front . . .
. . . I can start on the back . . .
. . . then we can meet in the middle!

They got to work.

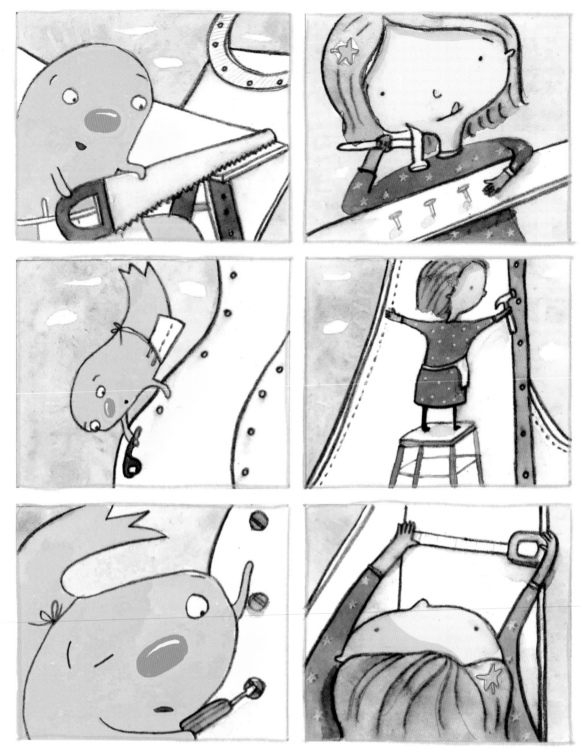

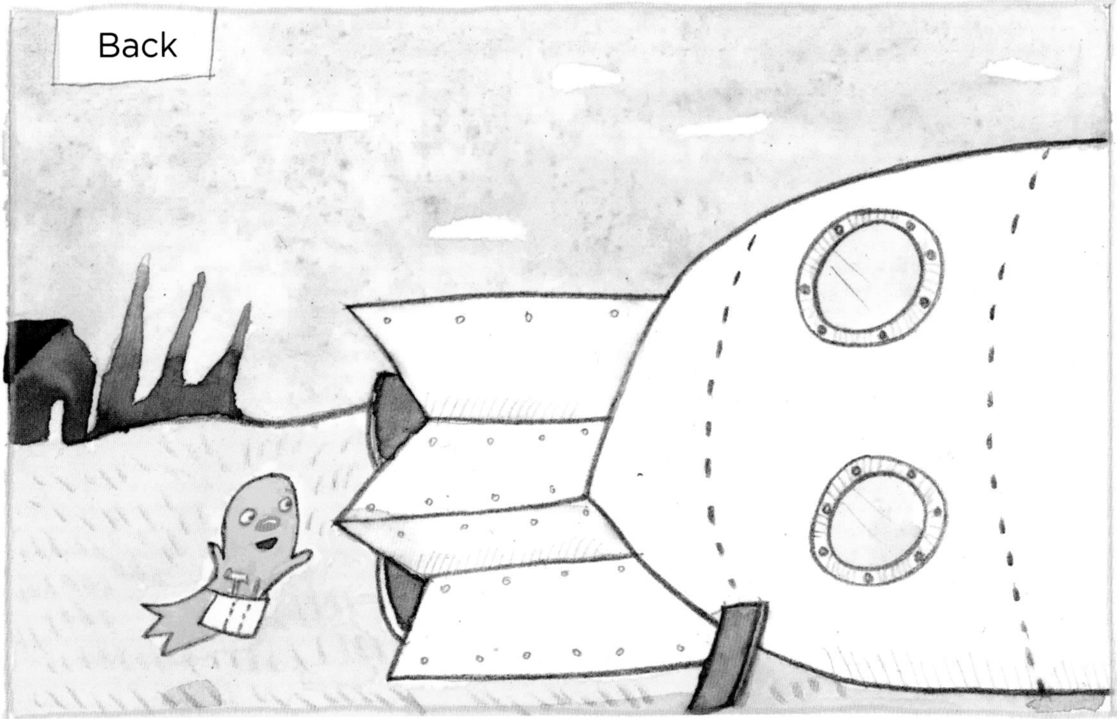
Back

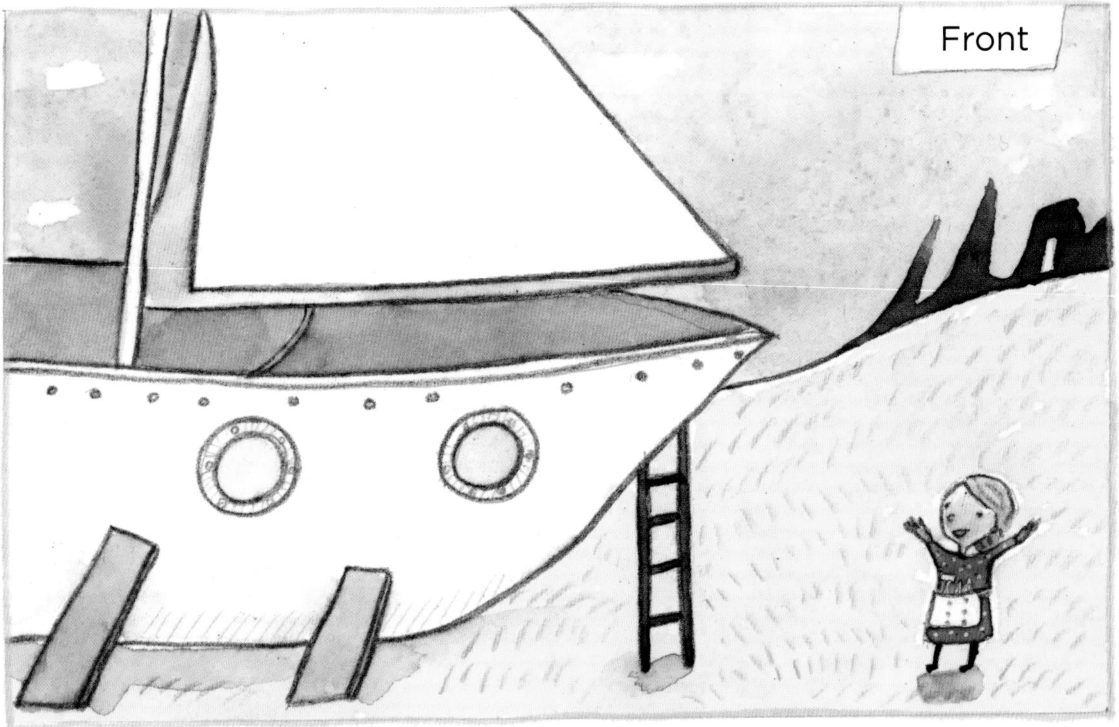
Front

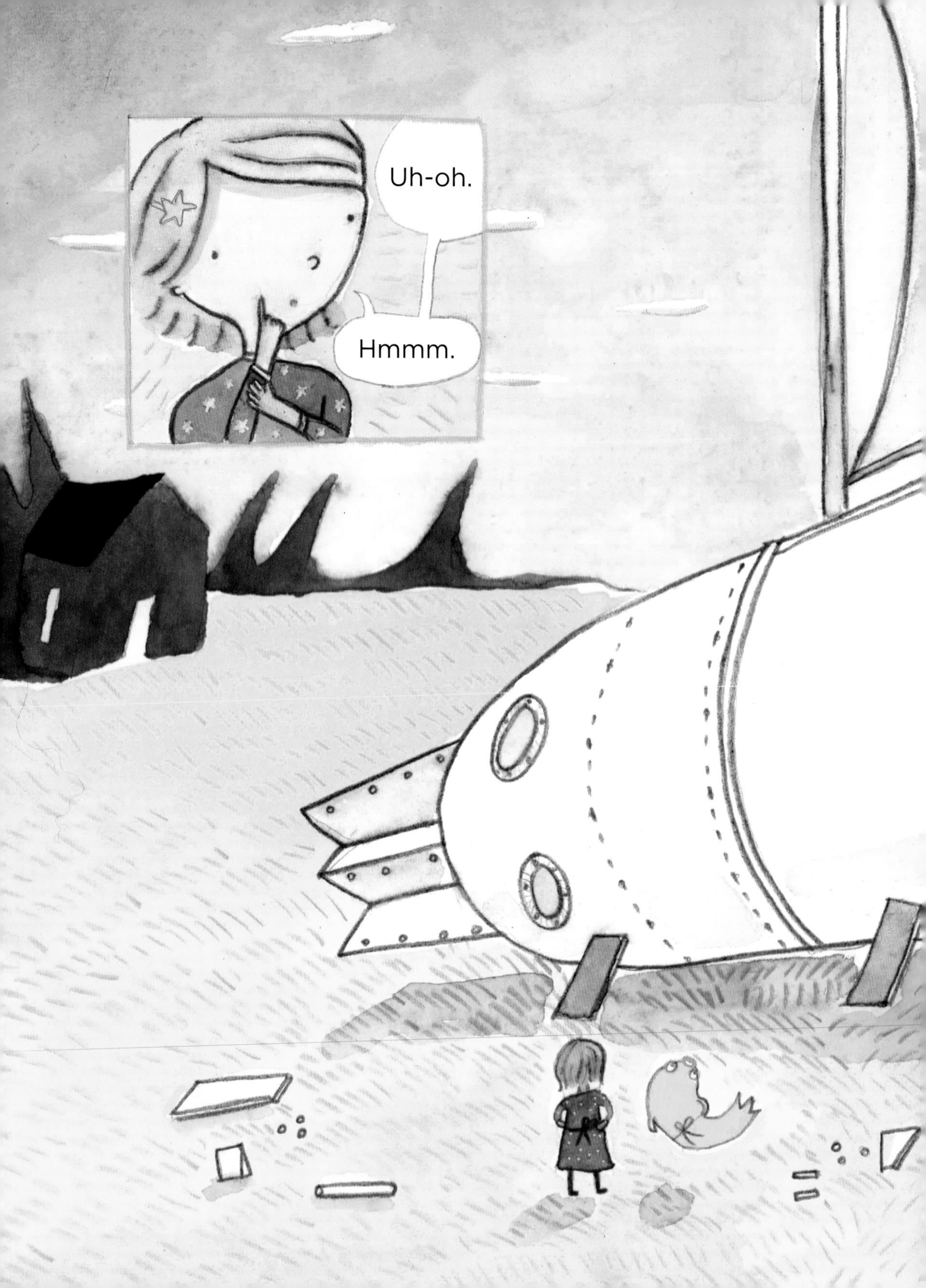
Uh-oh.
Hmmm.

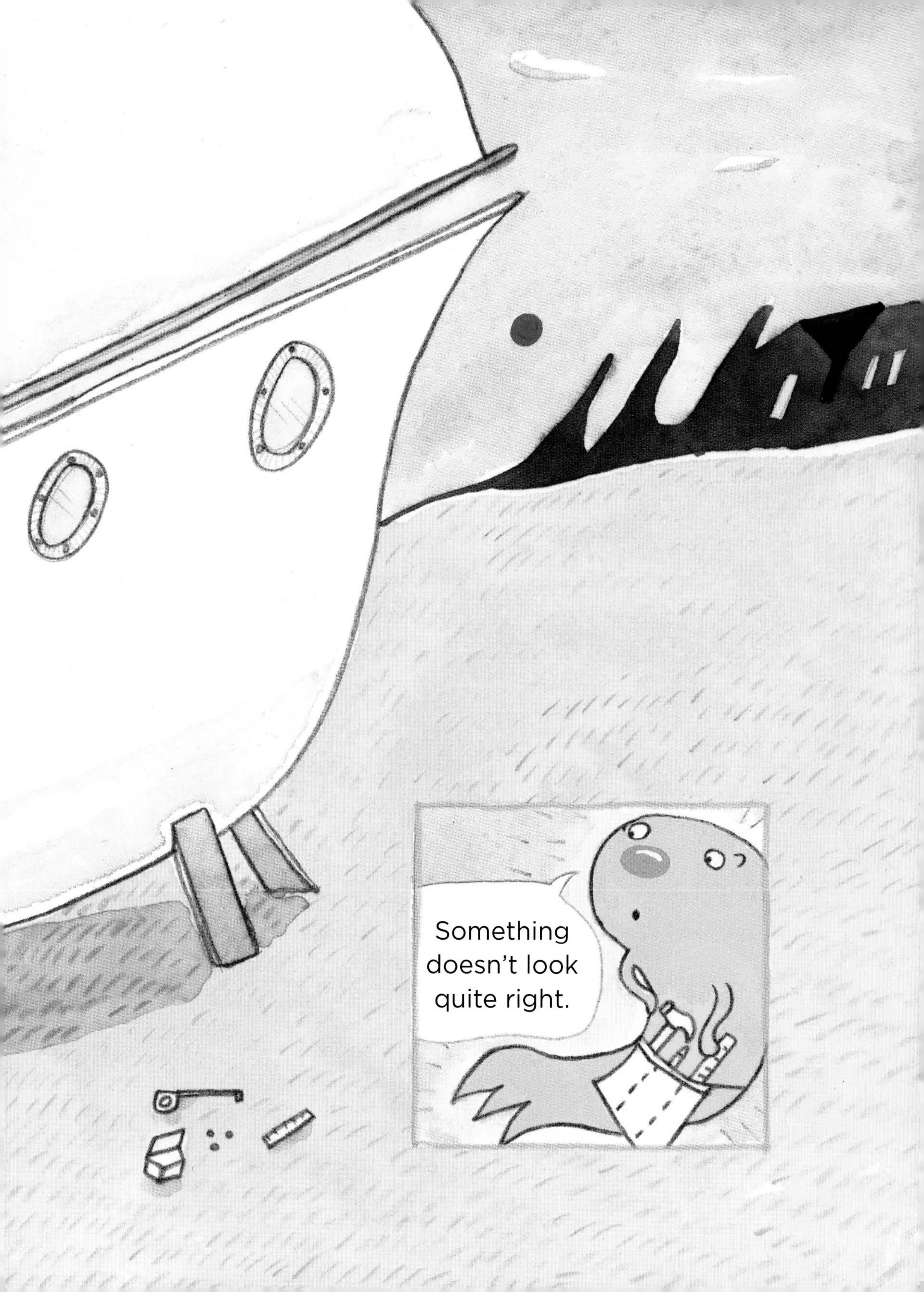
Something doesn't look quite right.

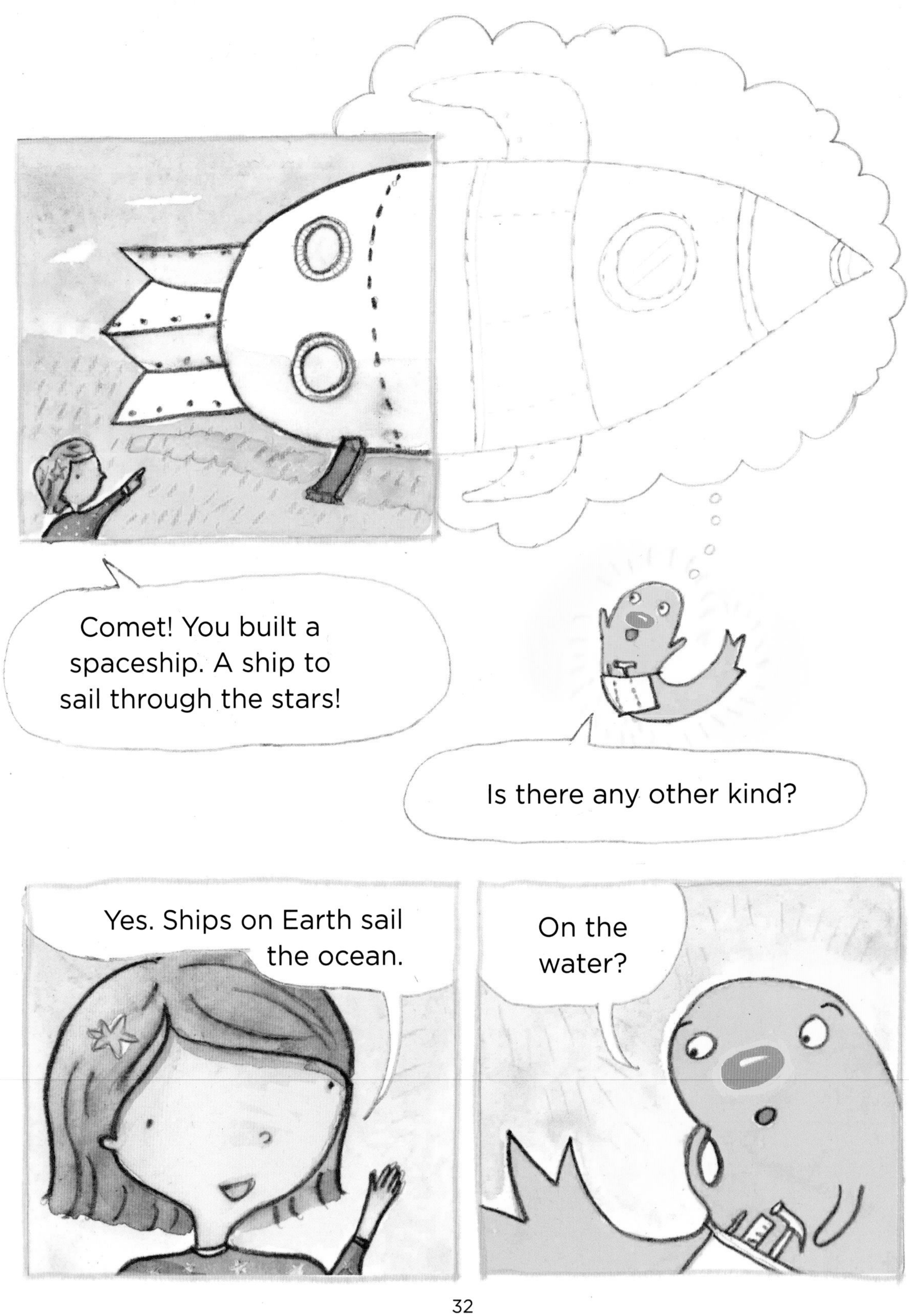
Comet! You built a spaceship. A ship to sail through the stars!
Is there any other kind?
Yes. Ships on Earth sail the ocean.
On the water?

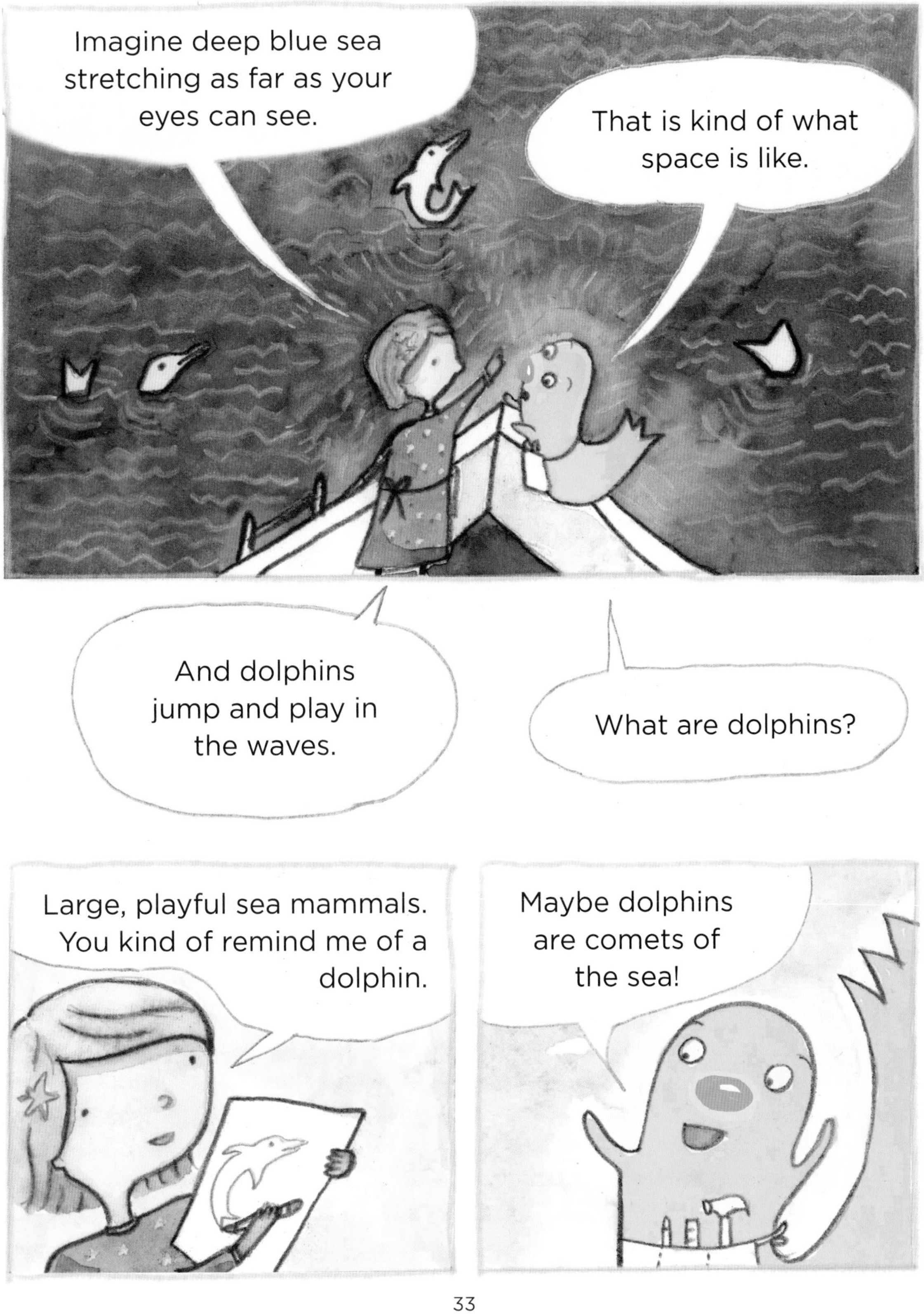
Imagine deep blue sea stretching as far as your eyes can see.
That is kind of what space is like.
And dolphins jump and play in the waves.
What are dolphins?
Large, playful sea mammals. You kind of remind me of a dolphin.
Maybe dolphins are comets of the sea!

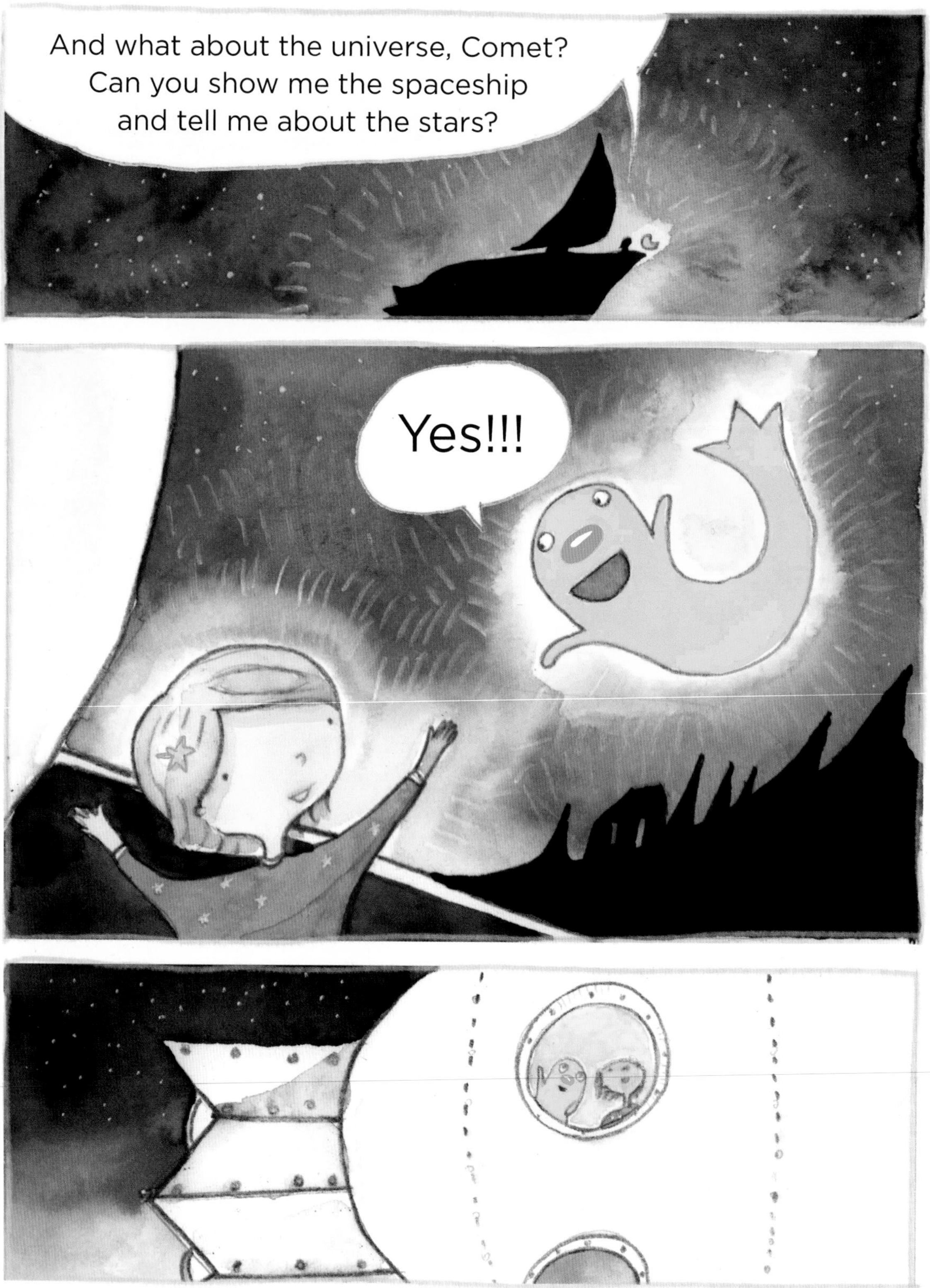
And what about the universe, Comet?
Can you show me the spaceship
and tell me about the stars?
Yes!!!

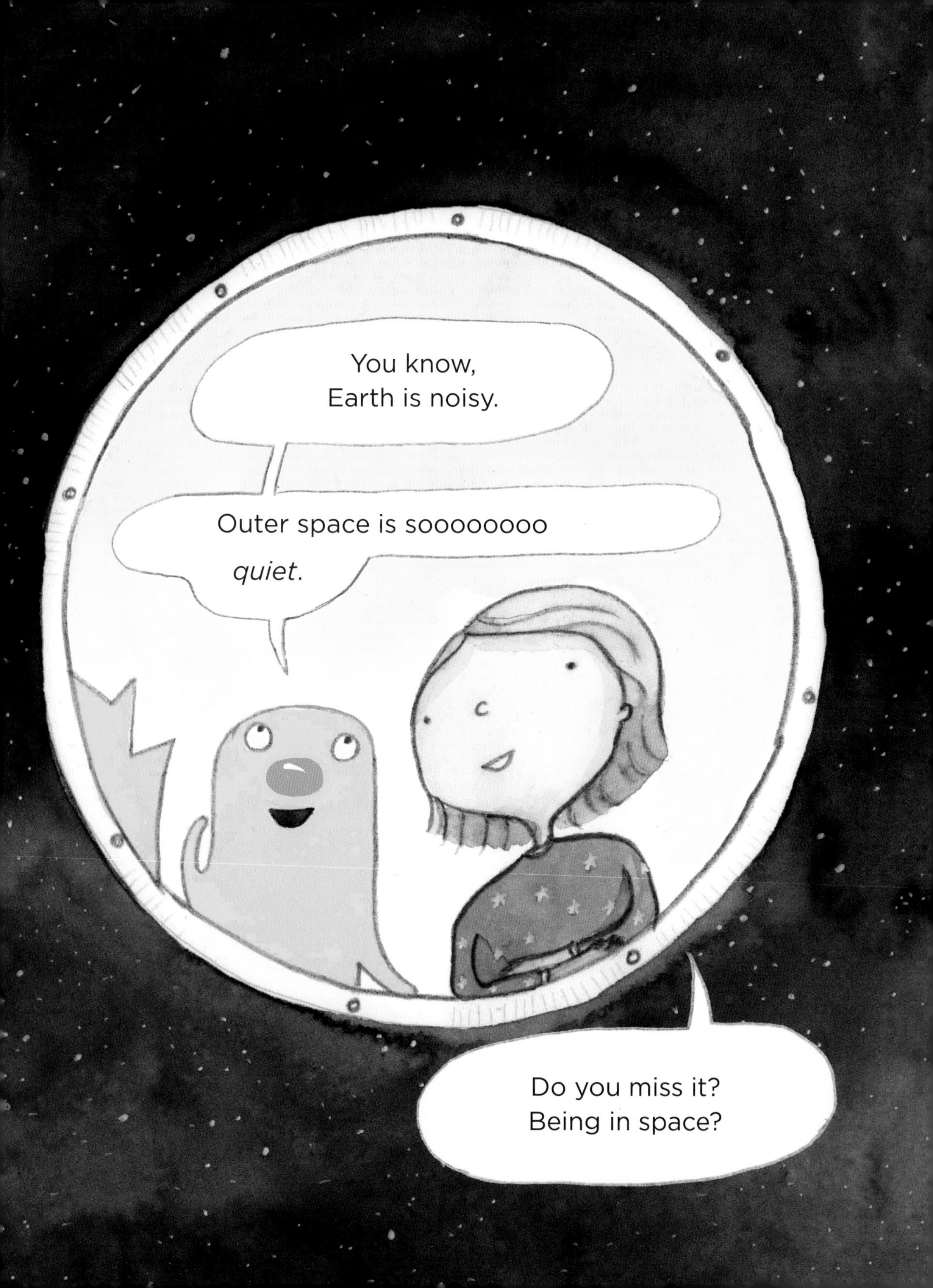
You know, Earth is noisy.
Outer space is soooooooo *quiet*.
Do you miss it? Being in space?

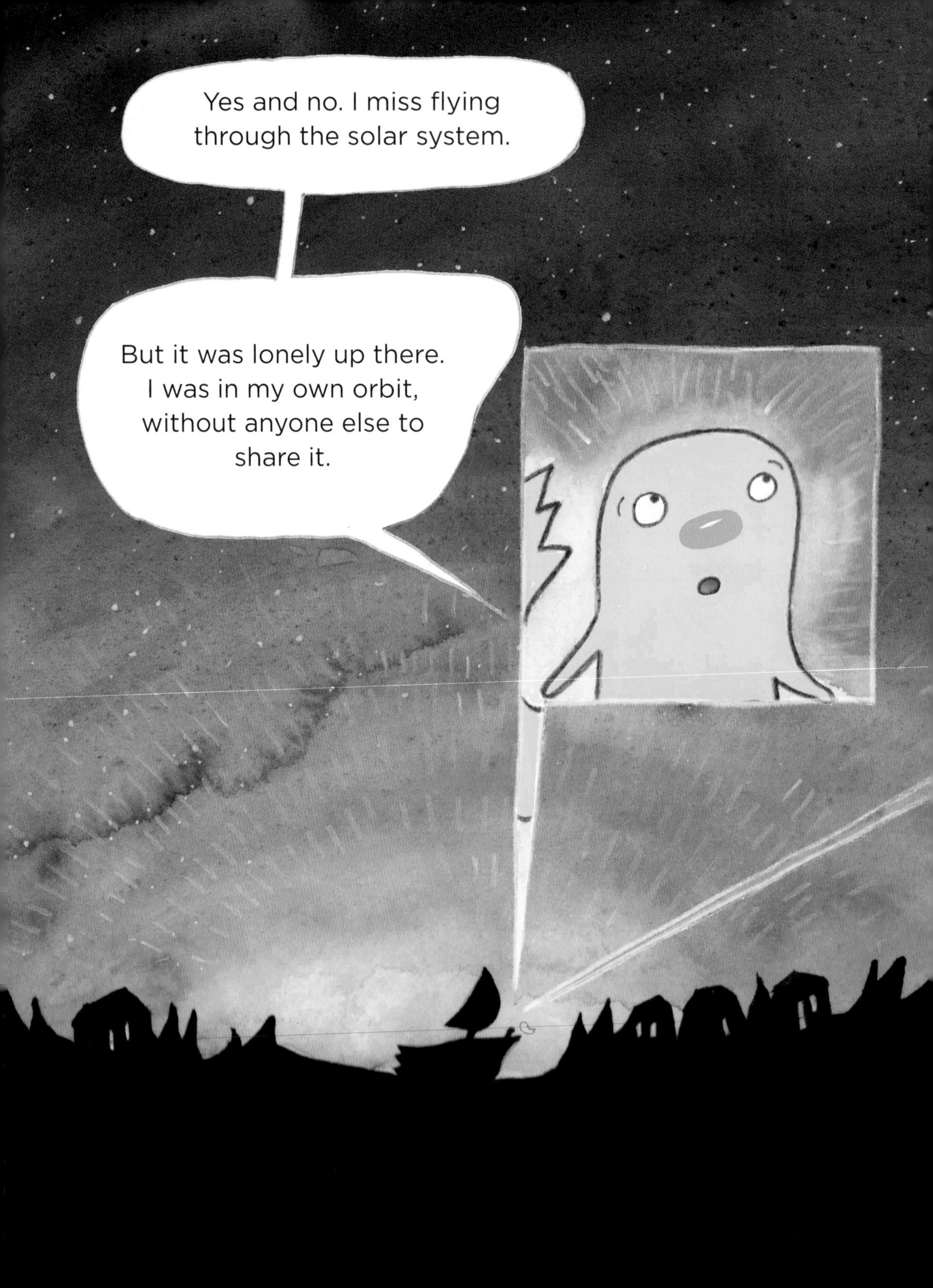
Yes and no. I miss flying through the solar system.
But it was lonely up there. I was in my own orbit, without anyone else to share it.

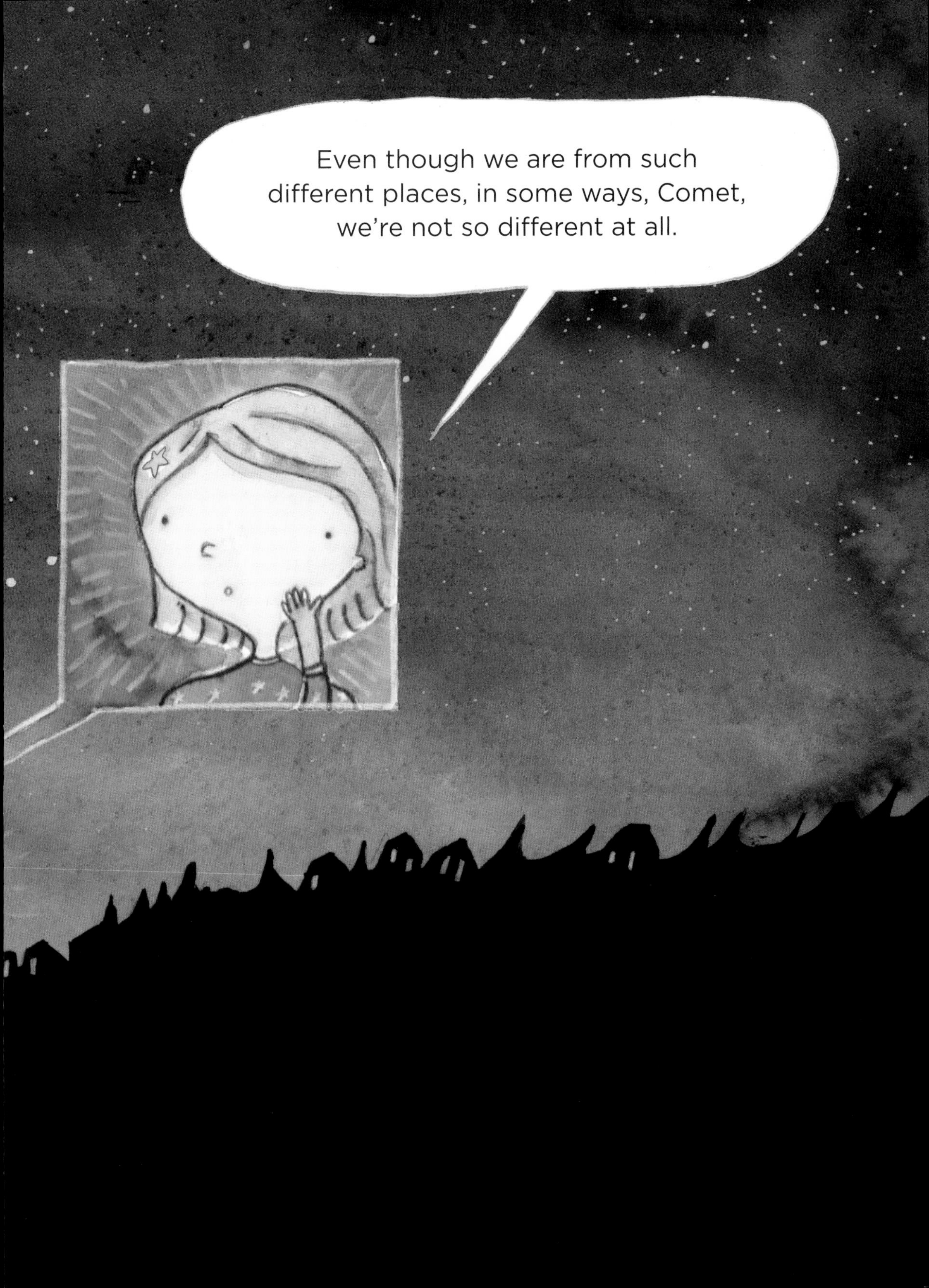
Even though we are from such different places, in some ways, Comet, we're not so different at all.

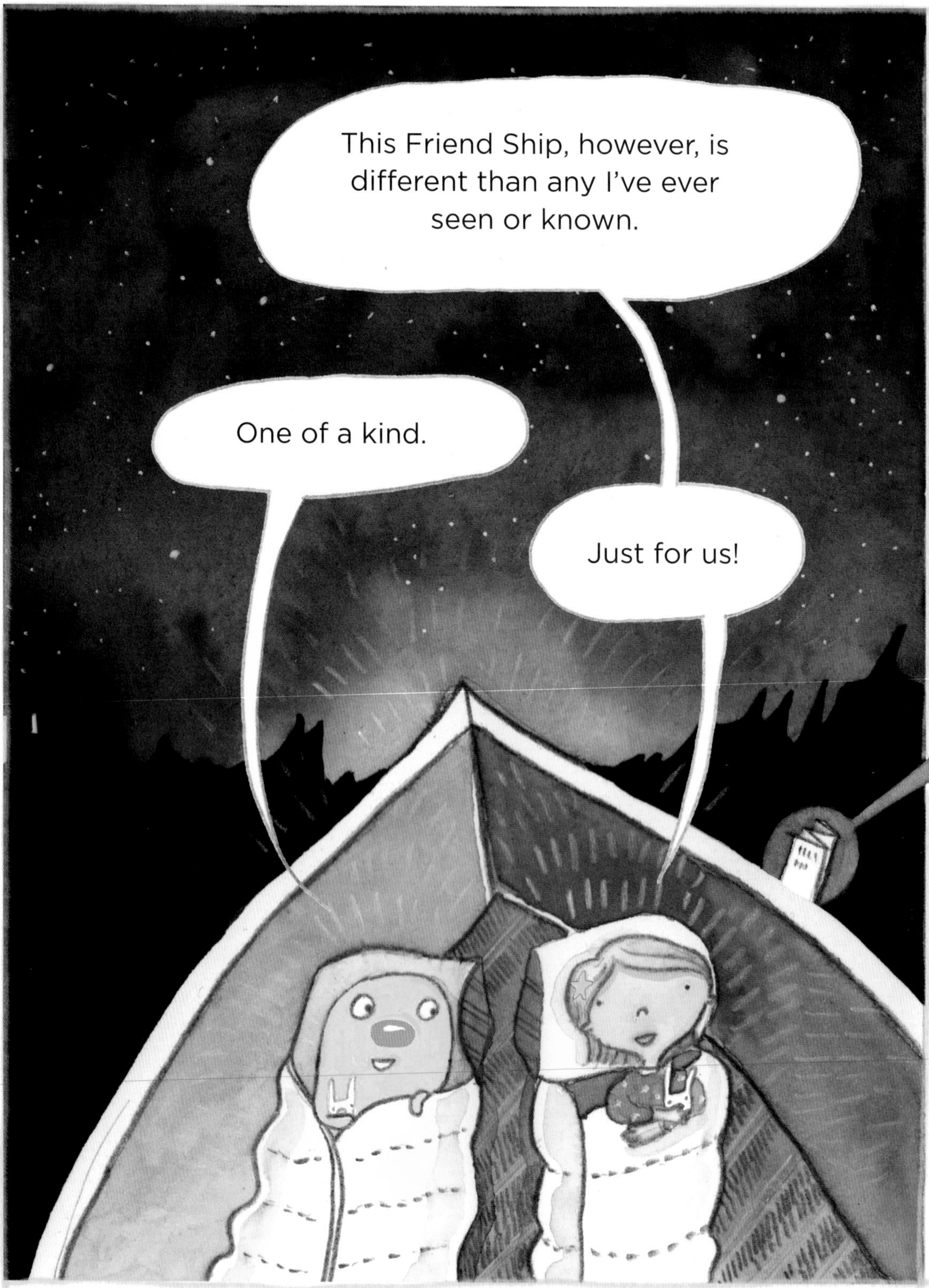
This Friend Ship, however, is different than any I've ever seen or known.
One of a kind.
Just for us!

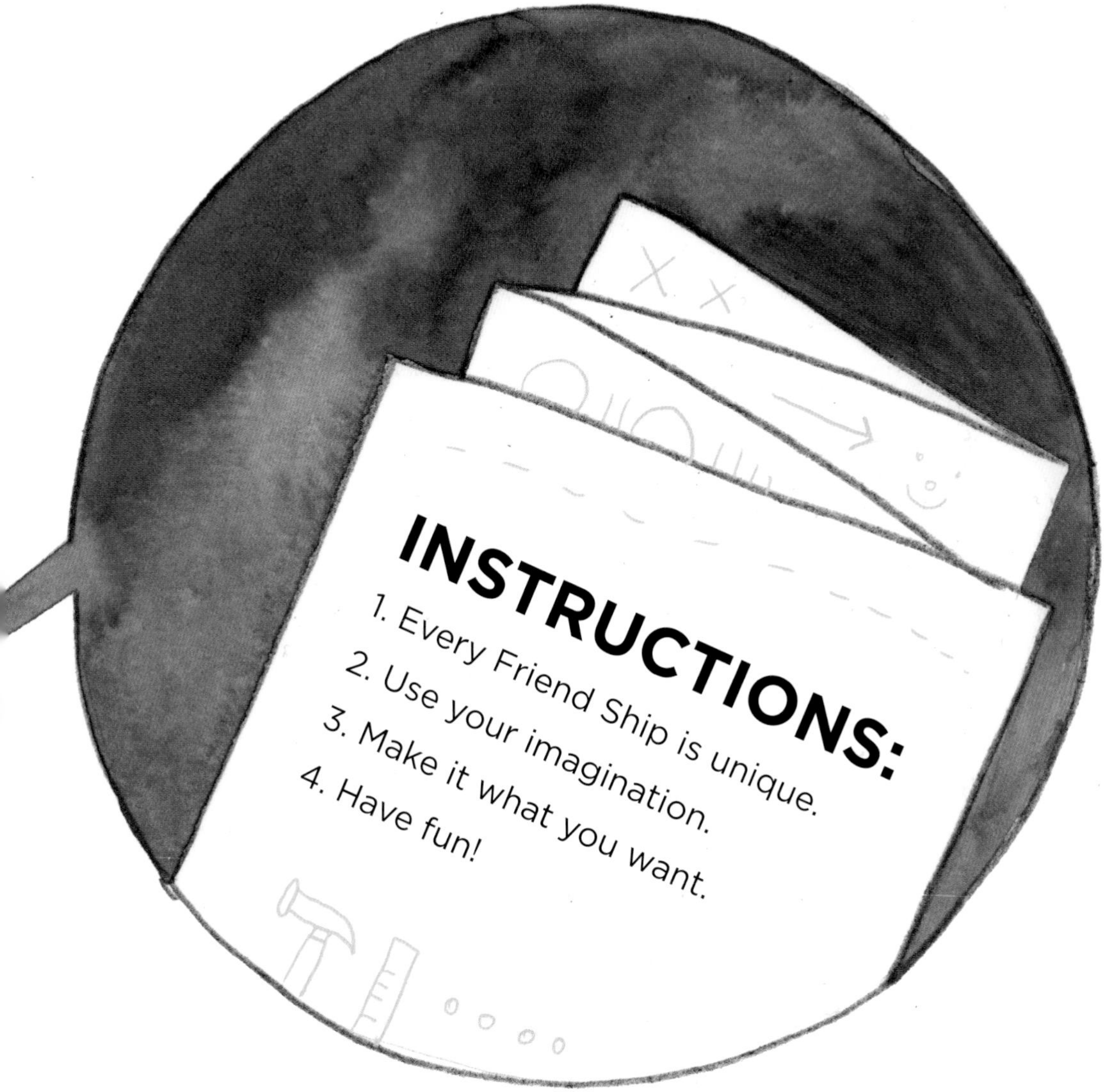
INSTRUCTIONS:
1. Every Friend Ship is unique.
2. Use your imagination.
3. Make it what you want.
4. Have fun!

Other kinds of ships that aren't ships but could be:

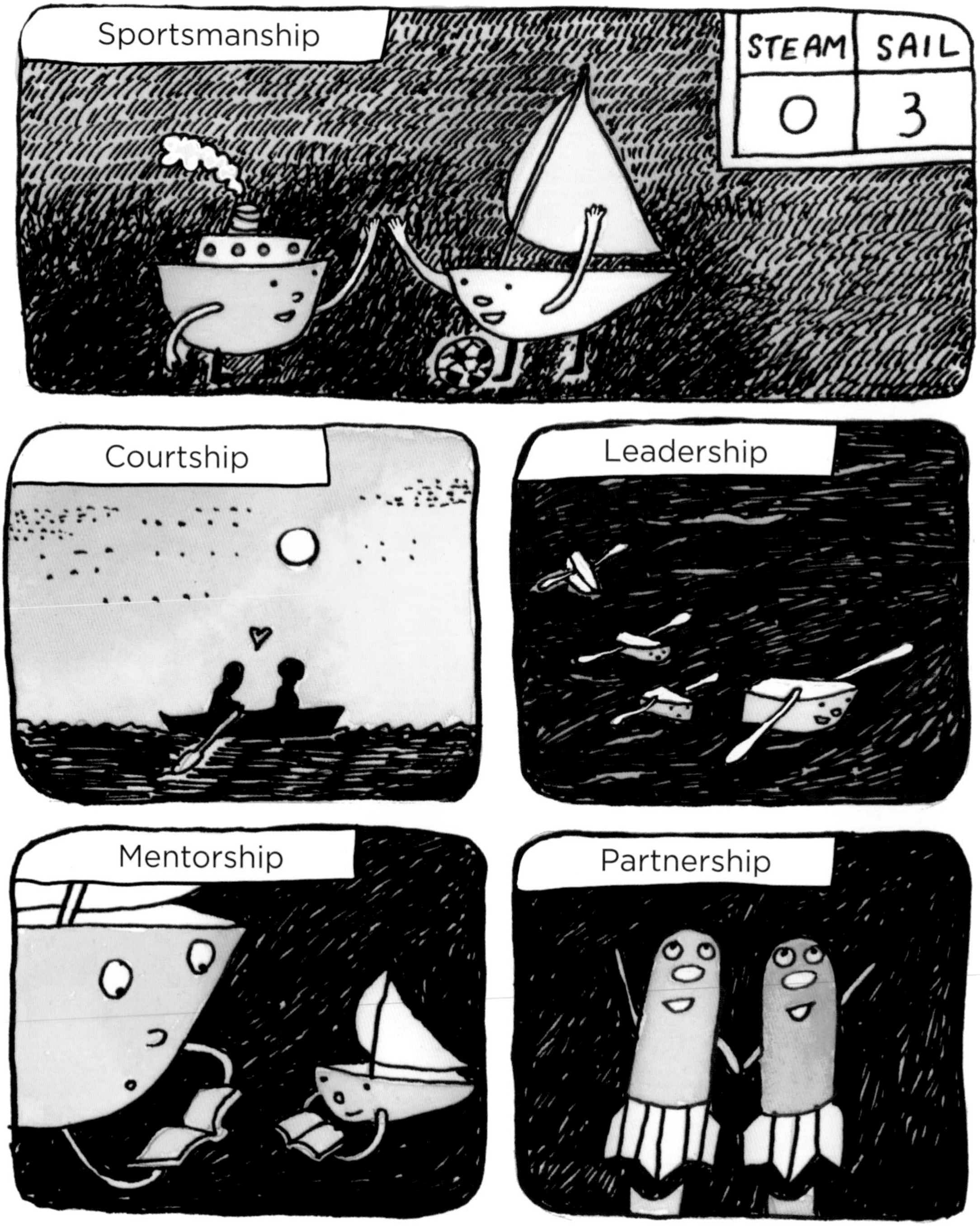
Sportsmanship
STEAM
SAIL
0
3
Courtship
Leadership
Mentorship
Partnership

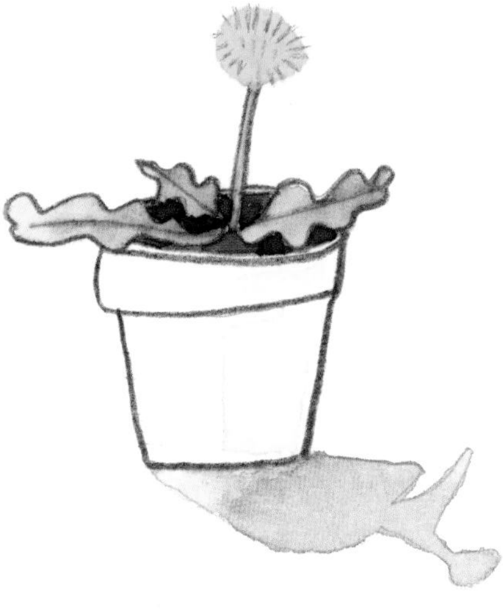

THE SURPRISE

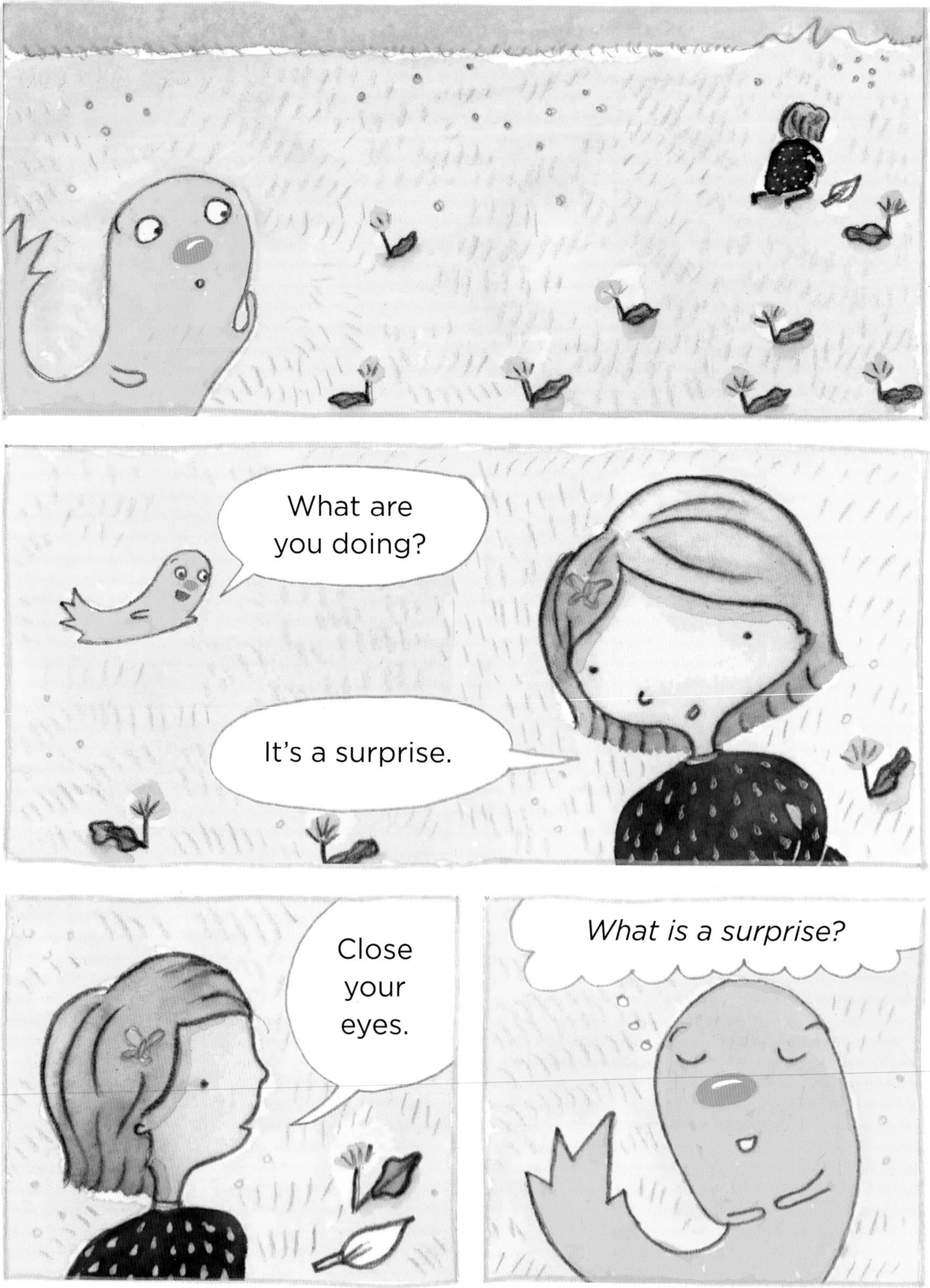
What are you doing?
It’s a surprise.
Close your eyes.
What is a surprise?

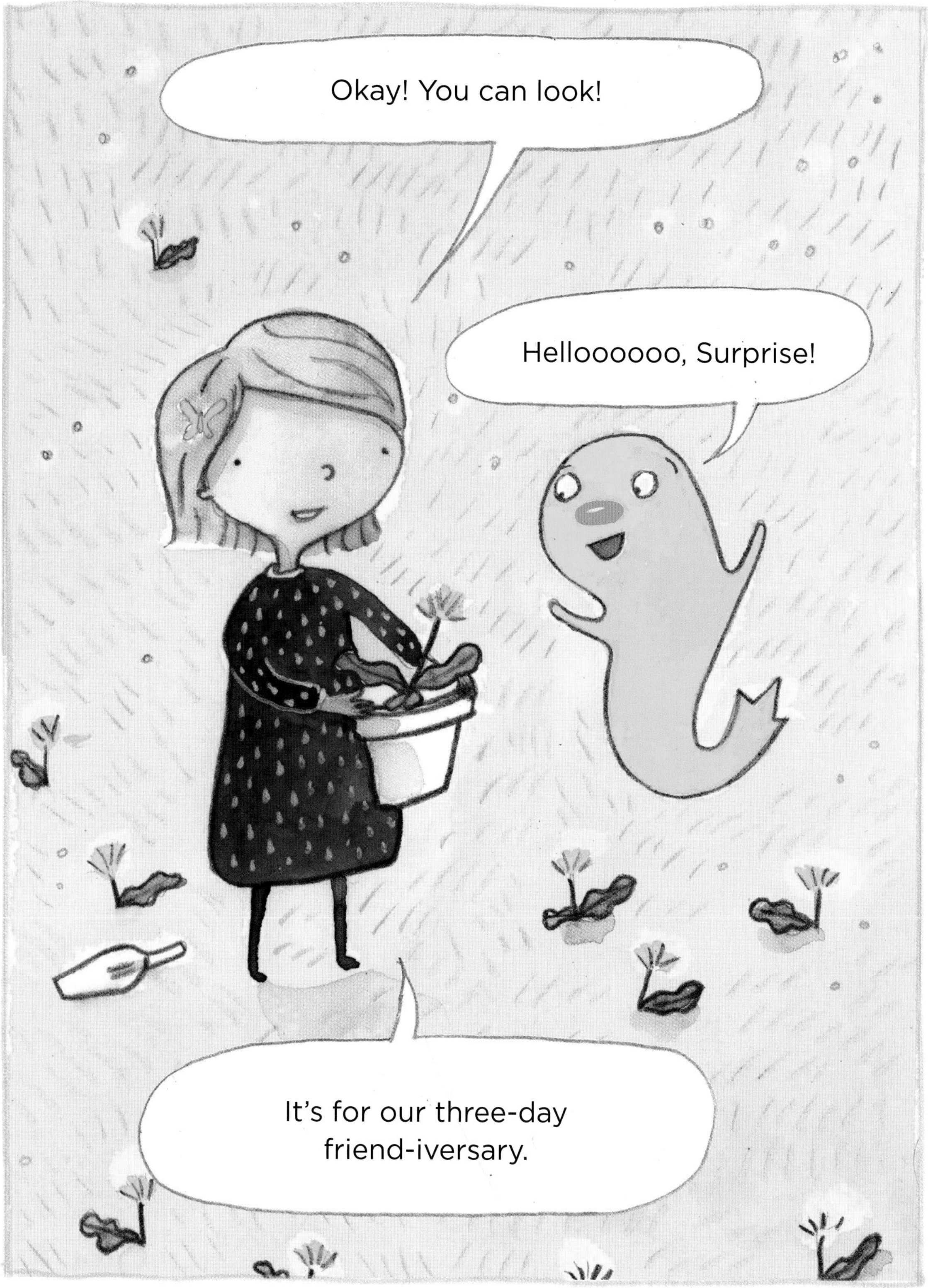
Okay! You can look!
Hellooooooo, Surprise!
It's for our three-day
friend-iversary.

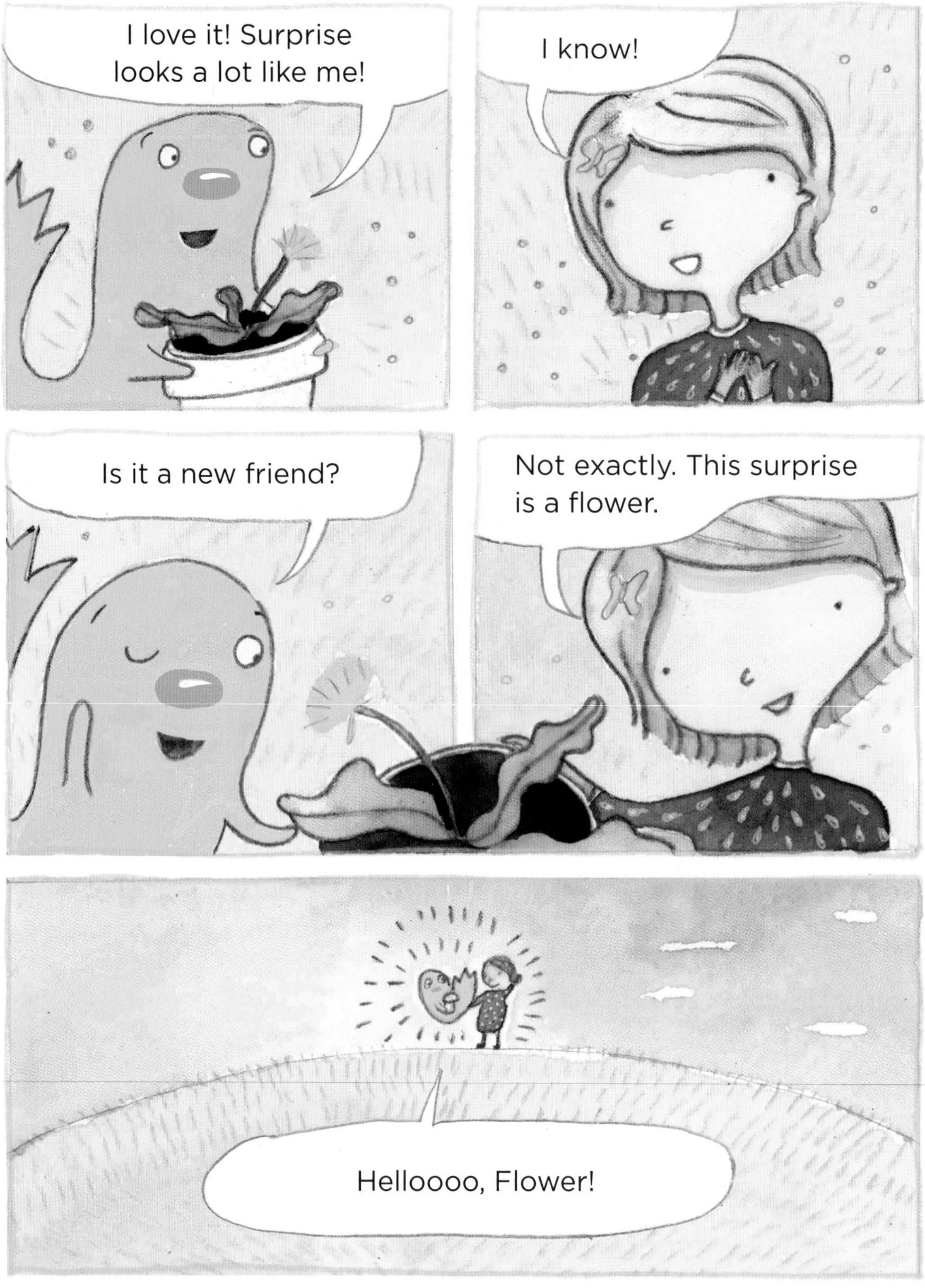
I love it! Surprise looks a lot like me!
I know!
Is it a new friend?
Not exactly. This surprise is a flower.
Helloooo, Flower!

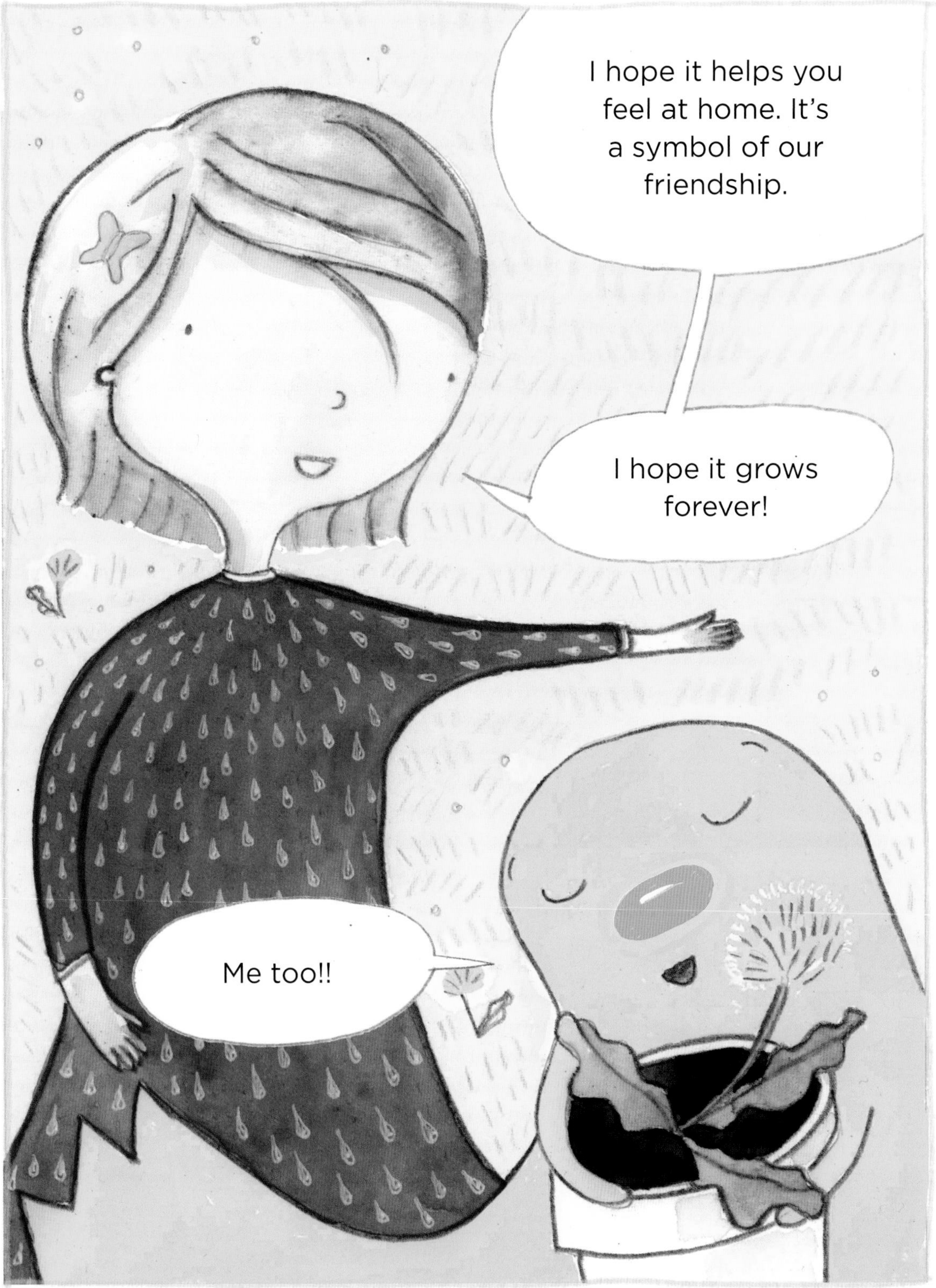
I hope it helps you feel at home. It's a symbol of our friendship.
I hope it grows forever!
Me too!!

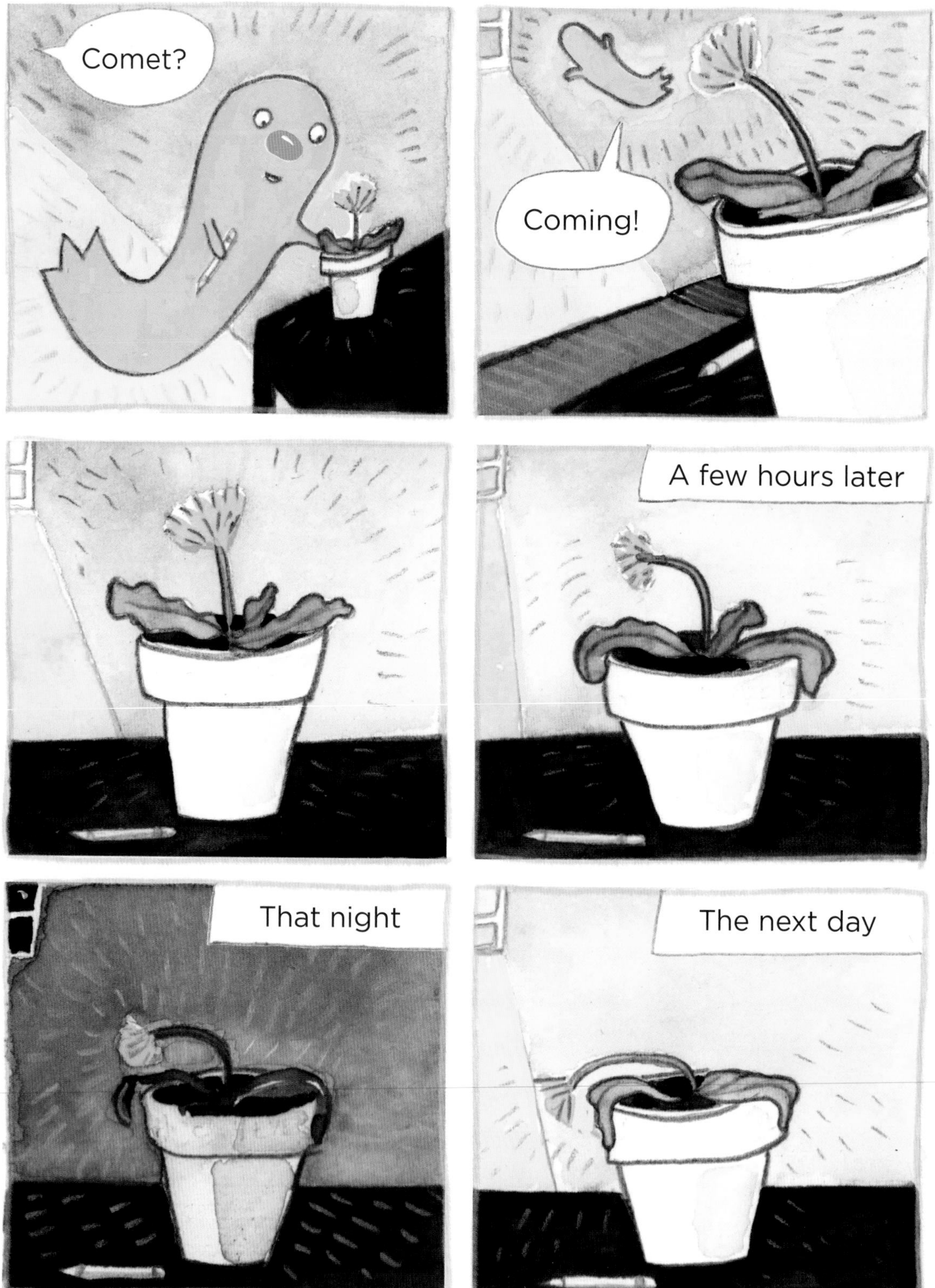
Comet?
Coming!
A few hours later
That night
The next day

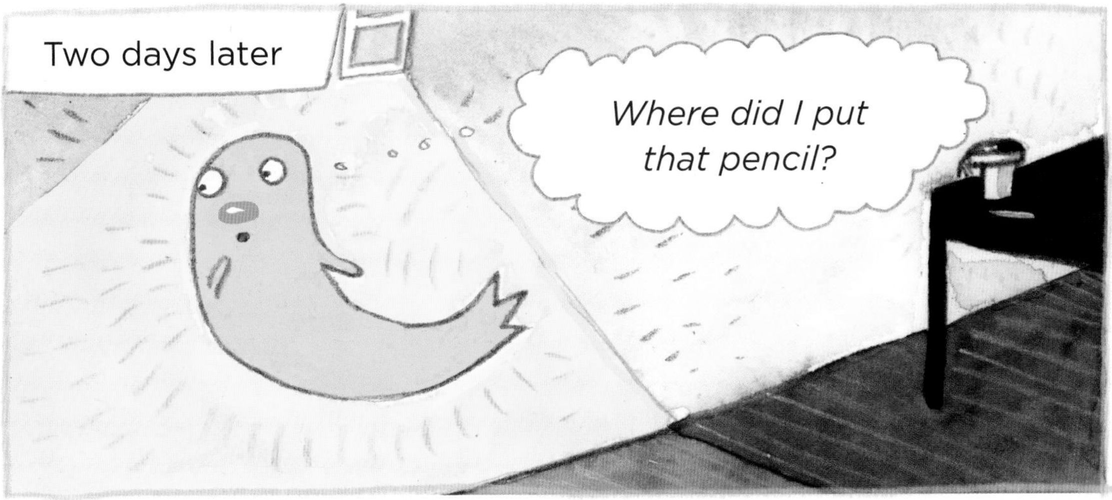
Two days later
Where did I put that pencil?

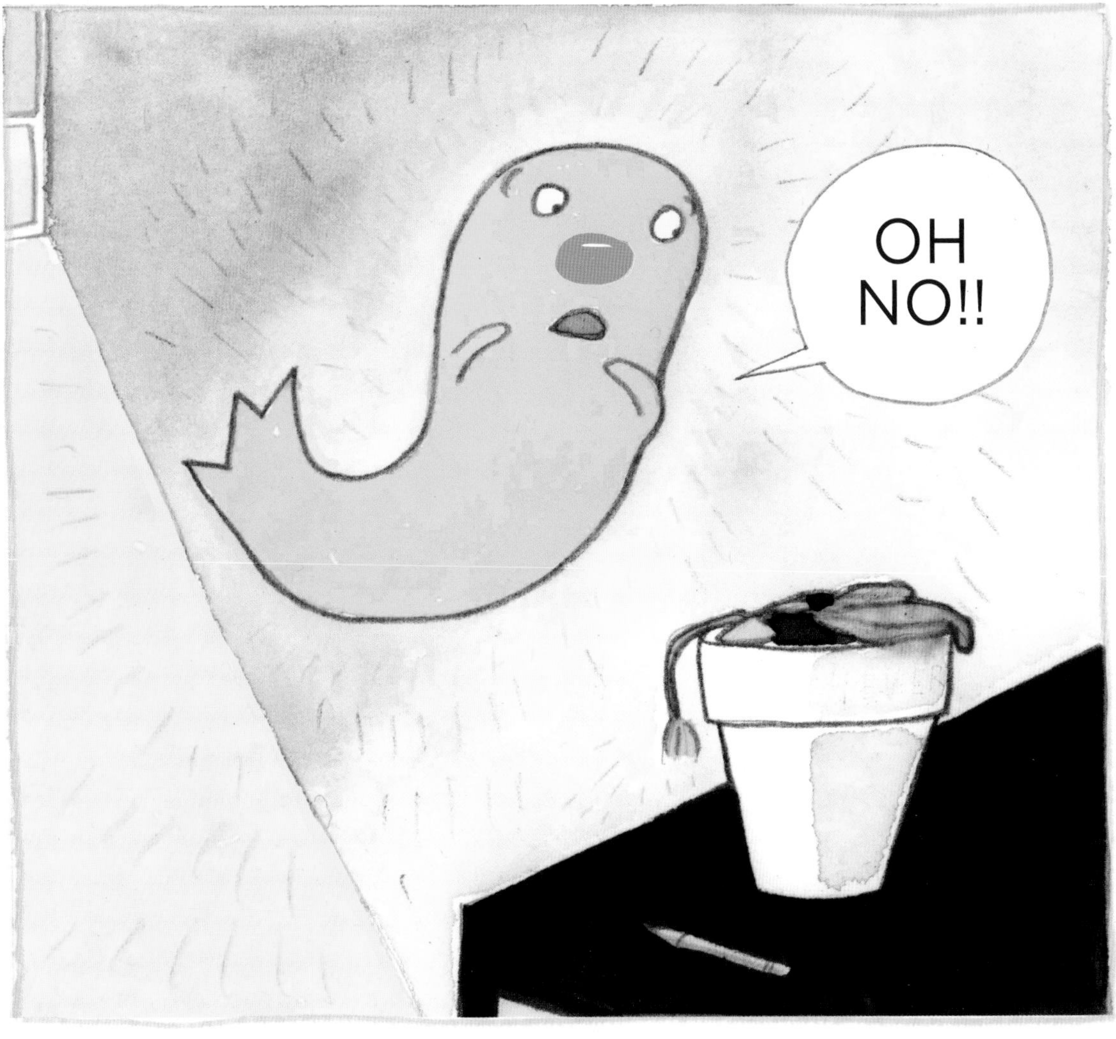
OH NO!!

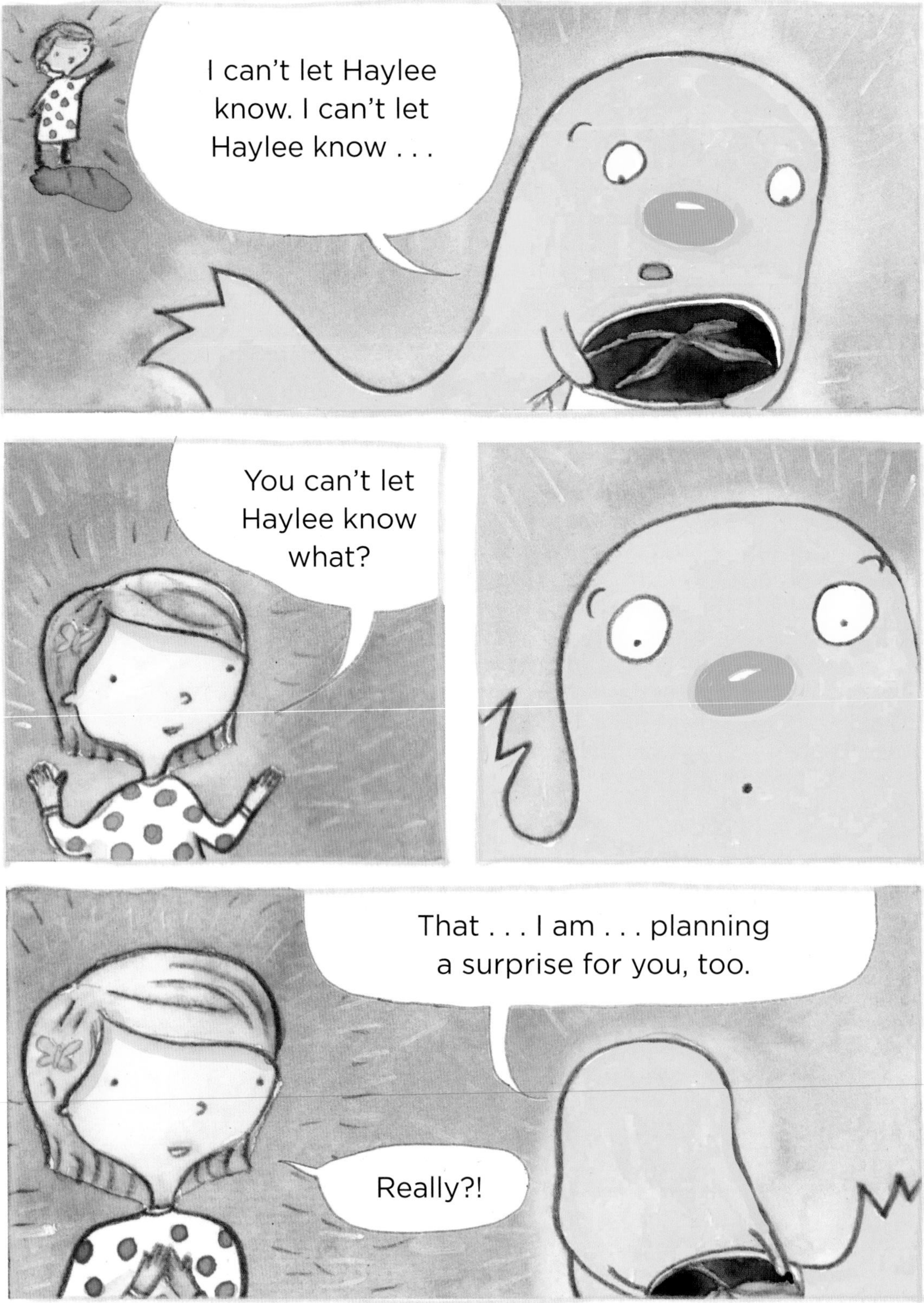
I can't let Haylee know. I can't let Haylee know . . .
You can't let Haylee know what?
That . . . I am . . . planning a surprise for you, too.
Really?!

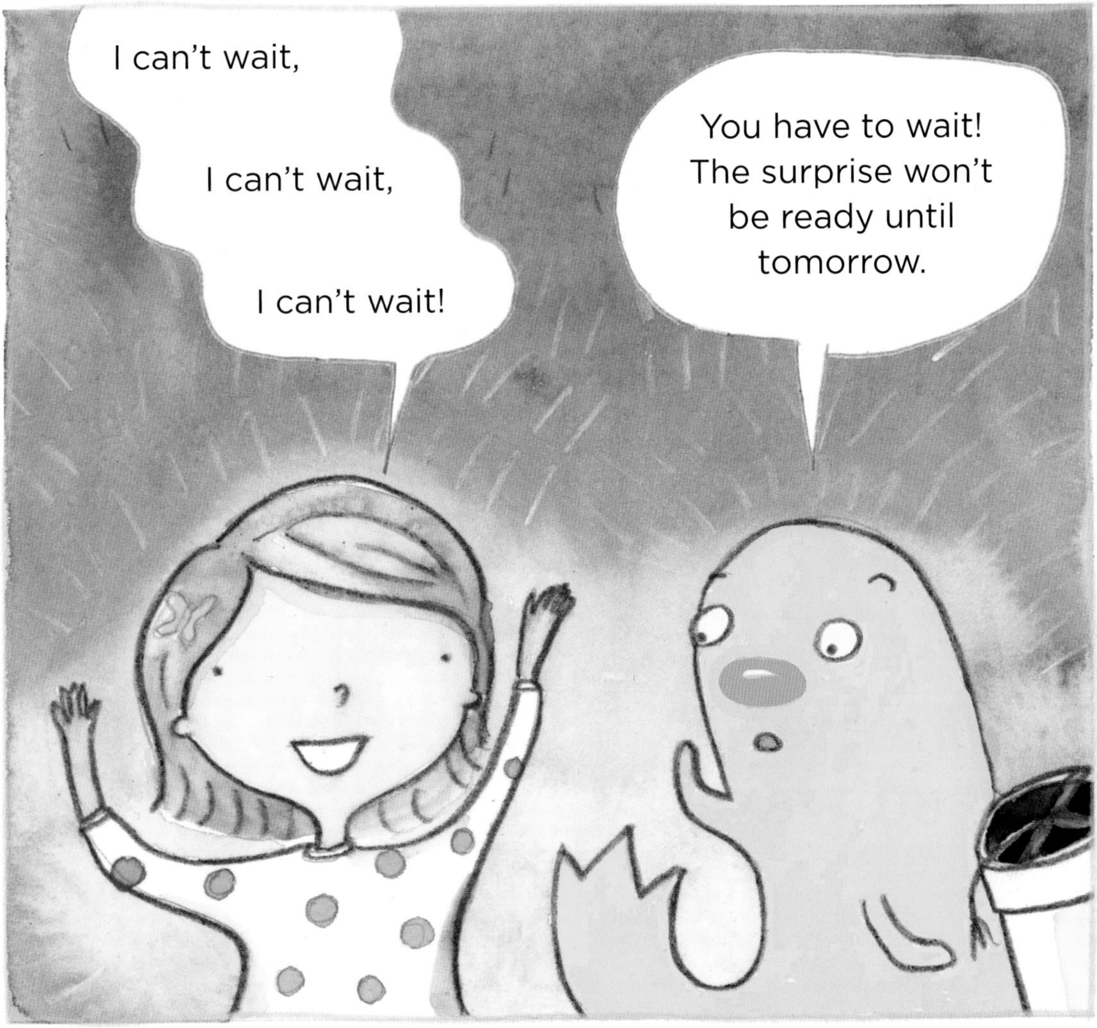
I can't wait,
I can't wait,
I can't wait!
You have to wait! The surprise won't be ready until tomorrow.

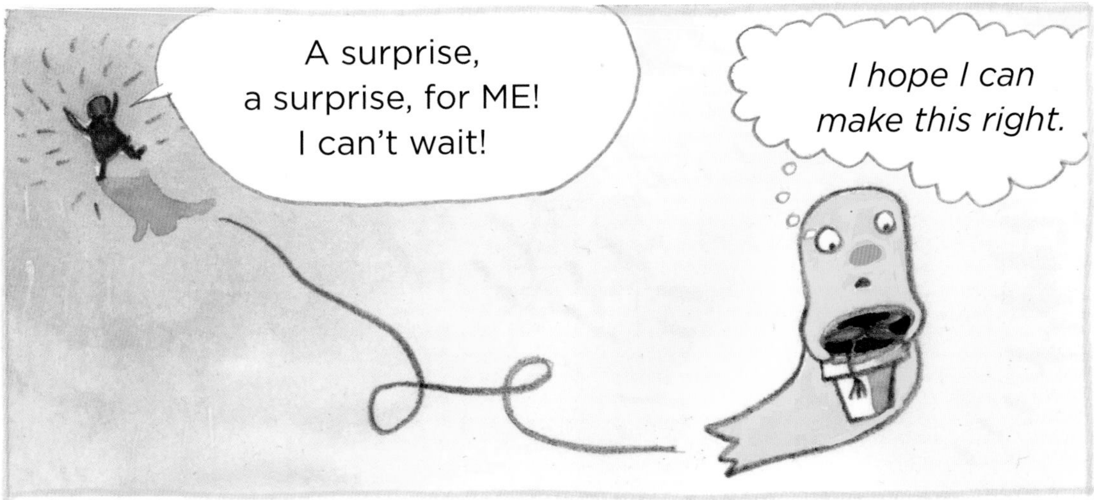
A surprise, a surprise, for ME! I can't wait!
I hope I can make this right.

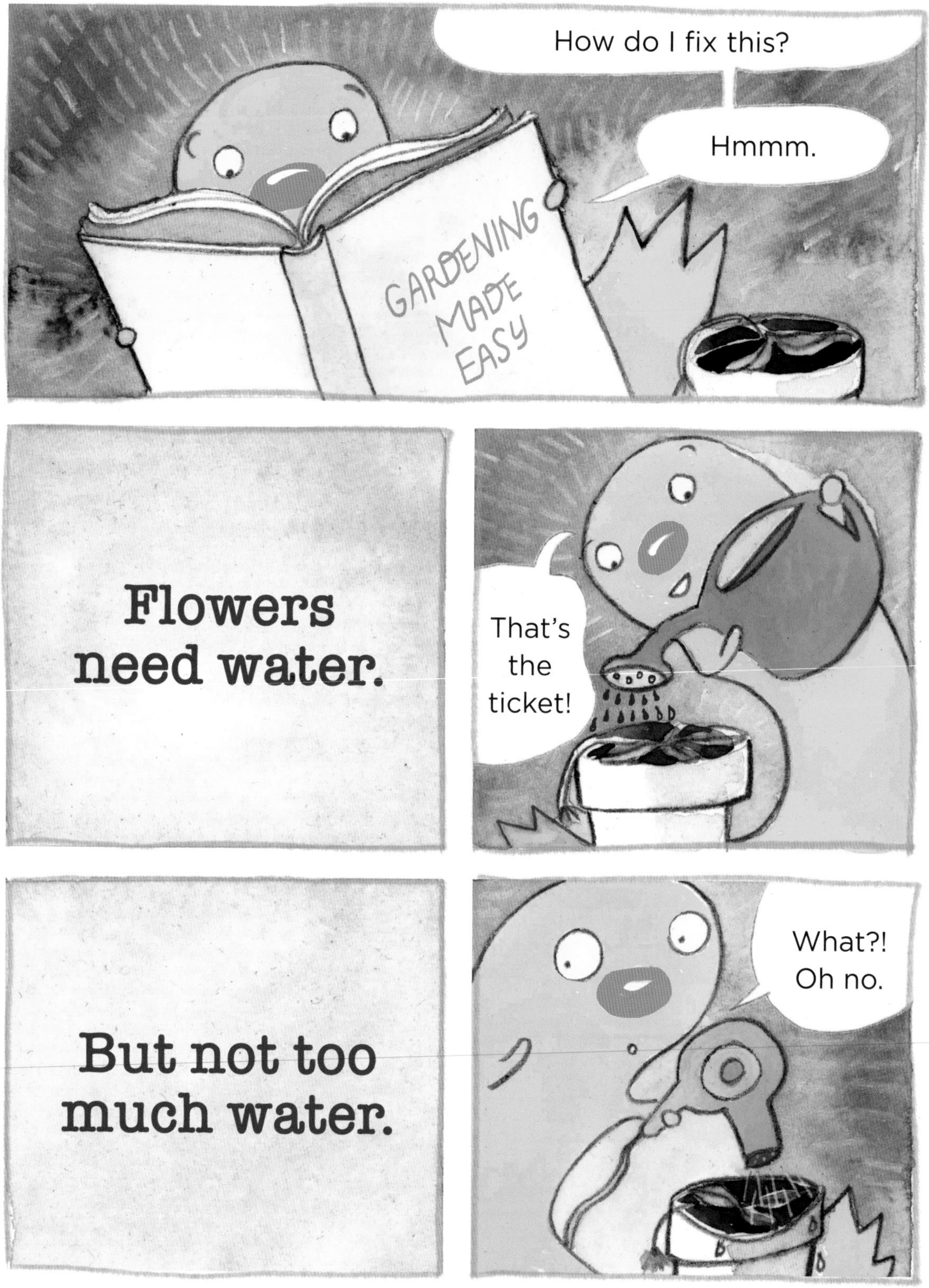
How do I fix this?
Hmmm.
GARDENING MADE EASY
Flowers need water.
That's the ticket!
But not too much water.
What?! Oh no.

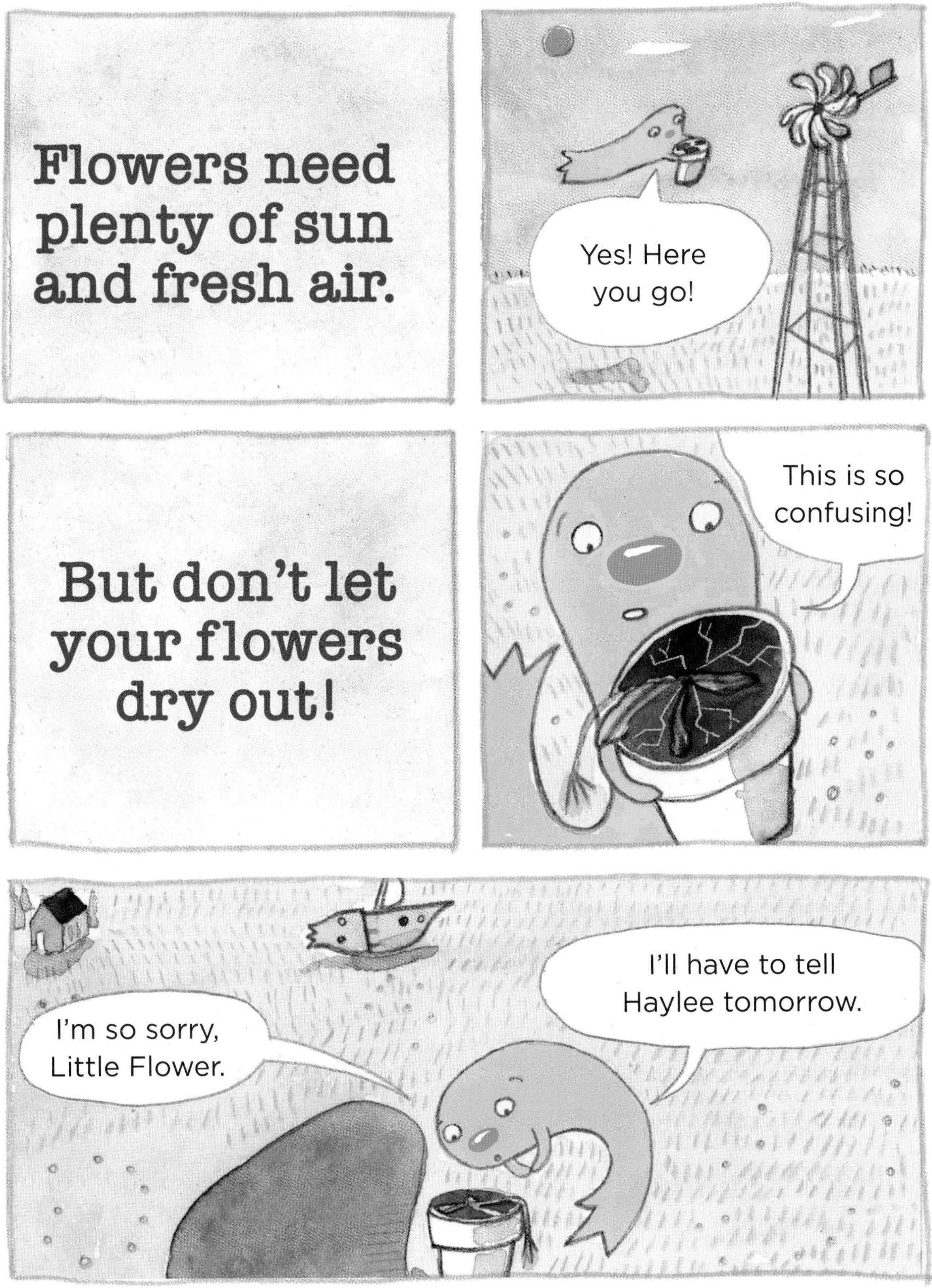
Flowers need plenty of sun and fresh air.
Yes! Here you go!
But don't let your flowers dry out!
This is so confusing!
I'm so sorry, Little Flower.
I'll have to tell Haylee tomorrow.

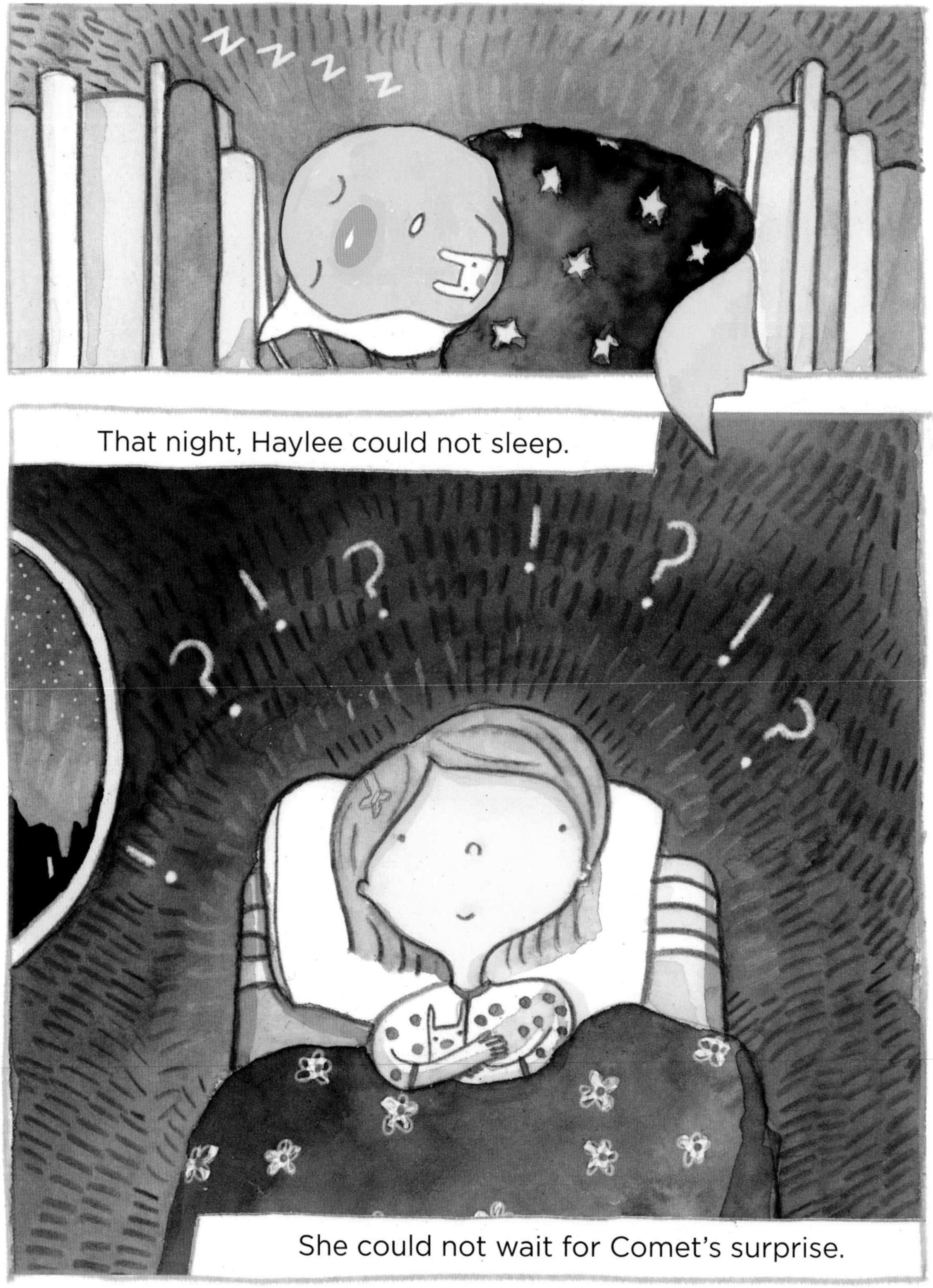
ZZZZ
That night, Haylee could not sleep.
She could not wait for Comet's surprise.

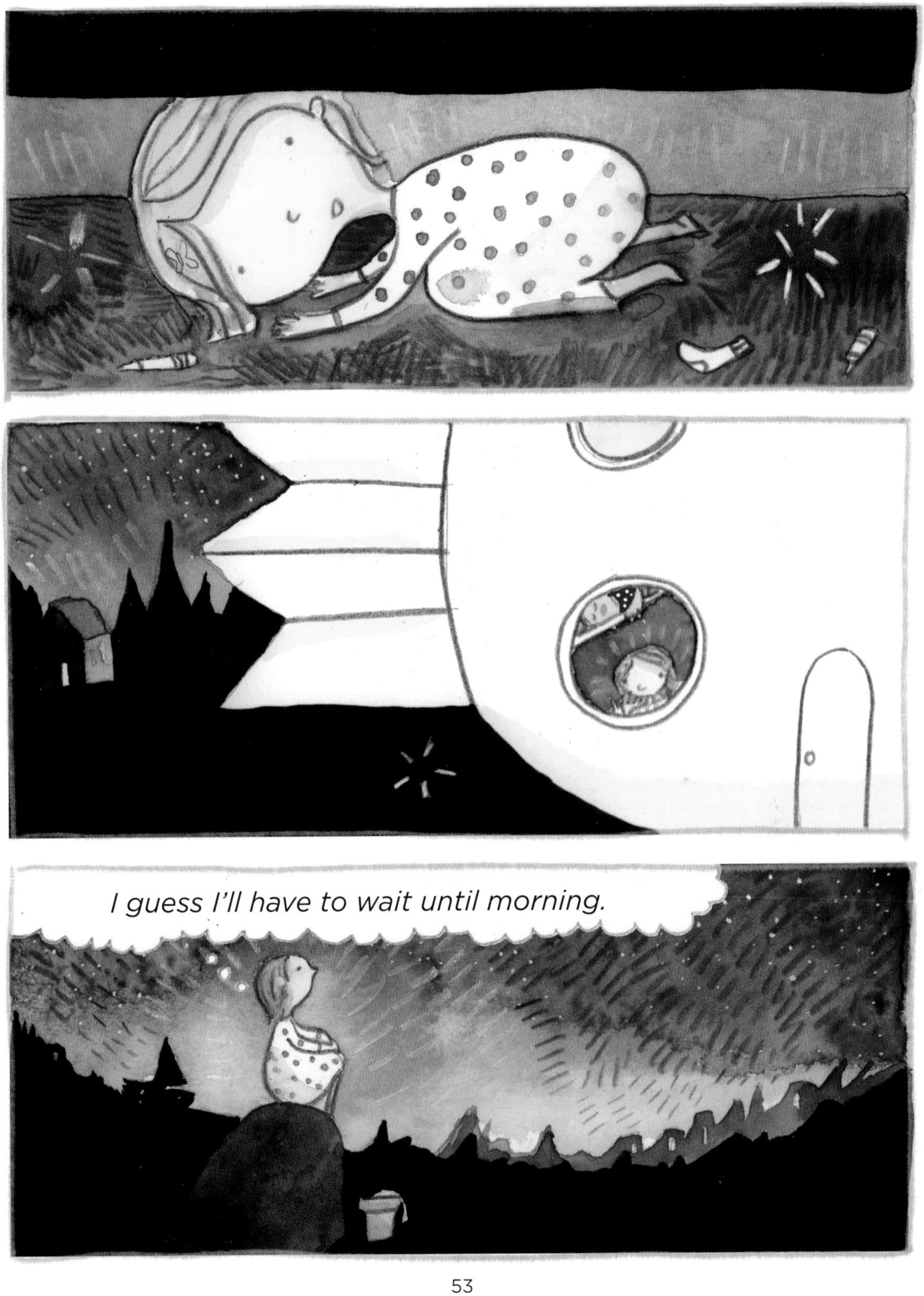
I guess I'll have to wait until morning.

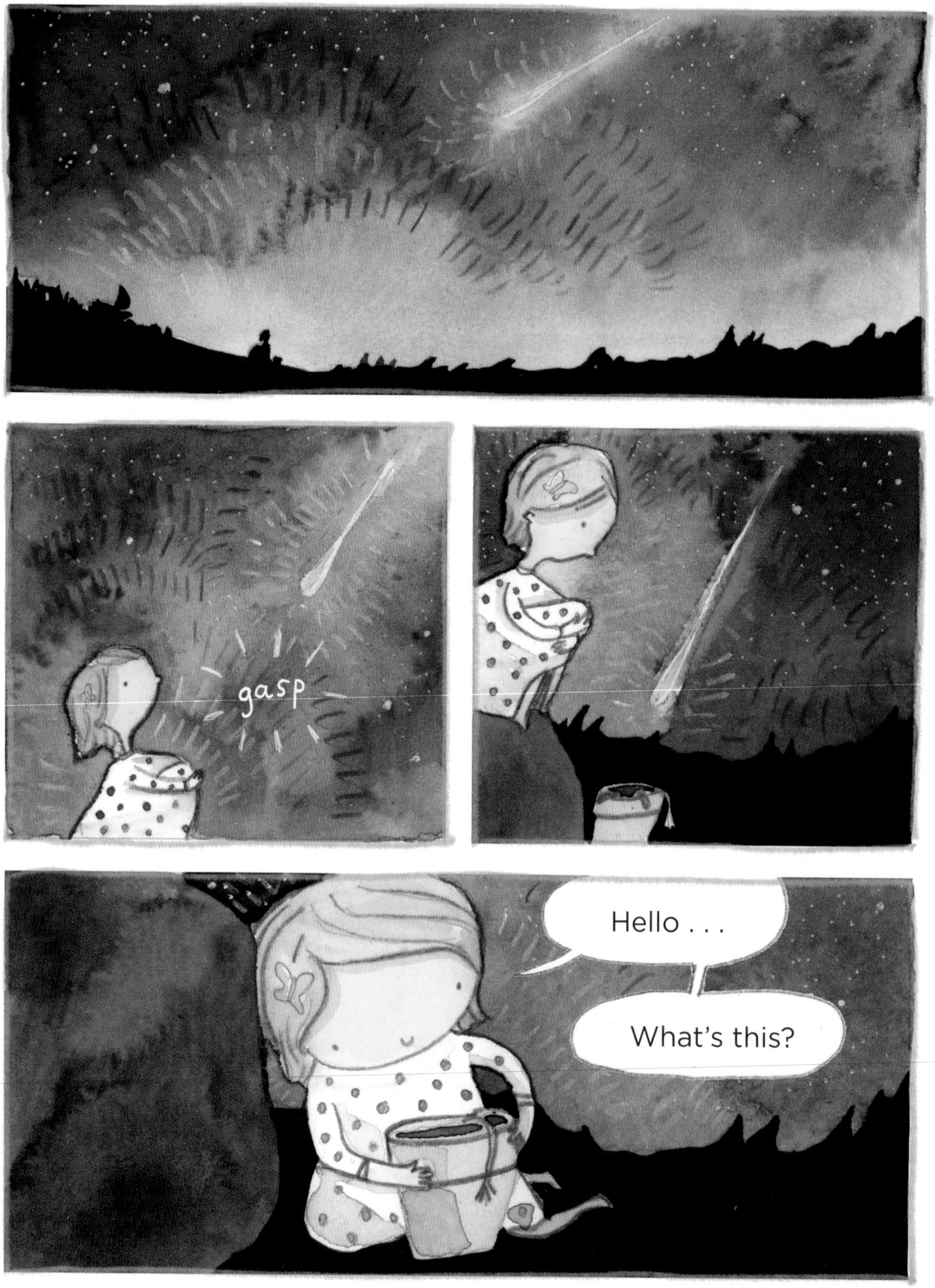
gasp
Hello . . .
What's this?

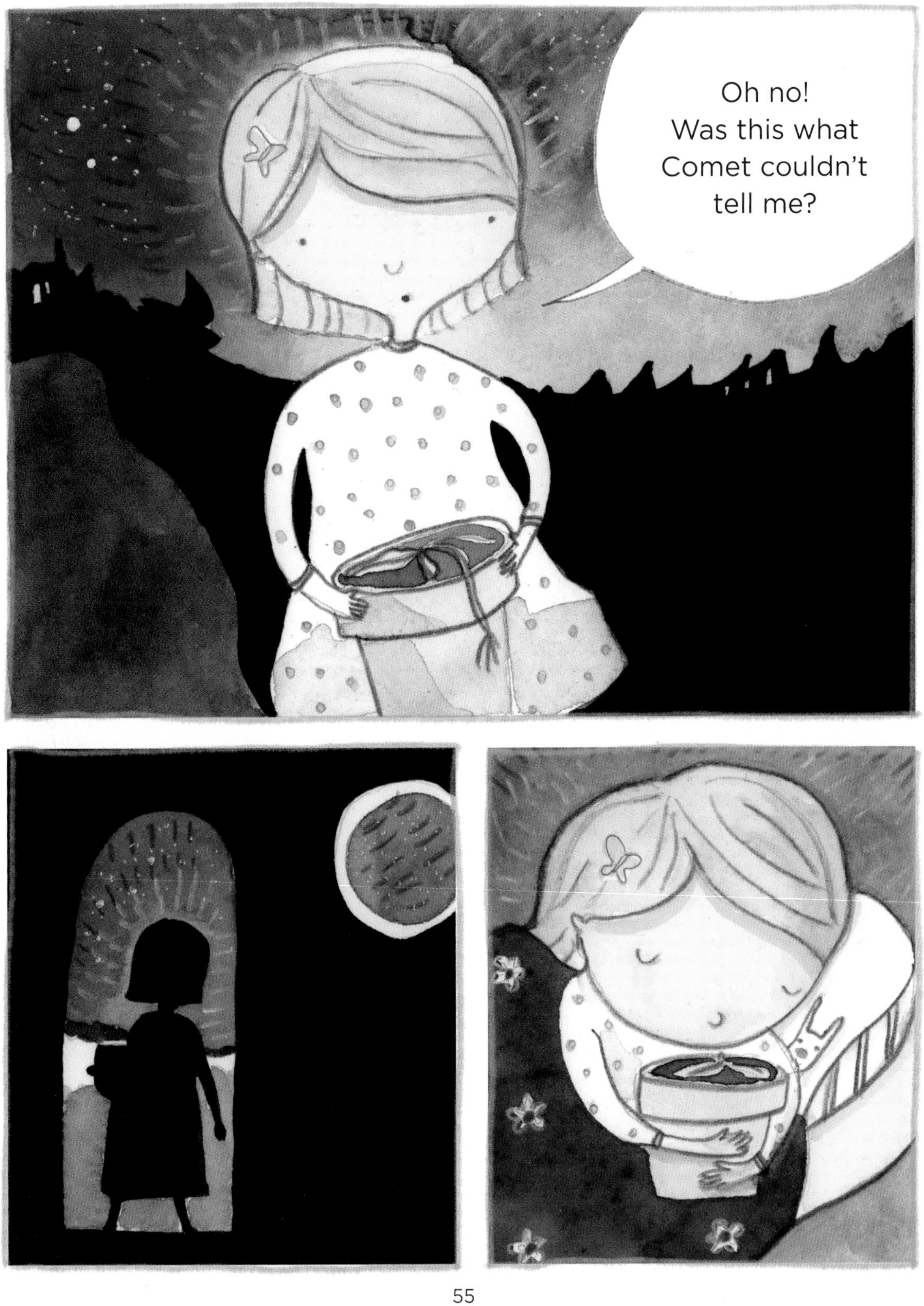
Oh no! Was this what Comet couldn't tell me?

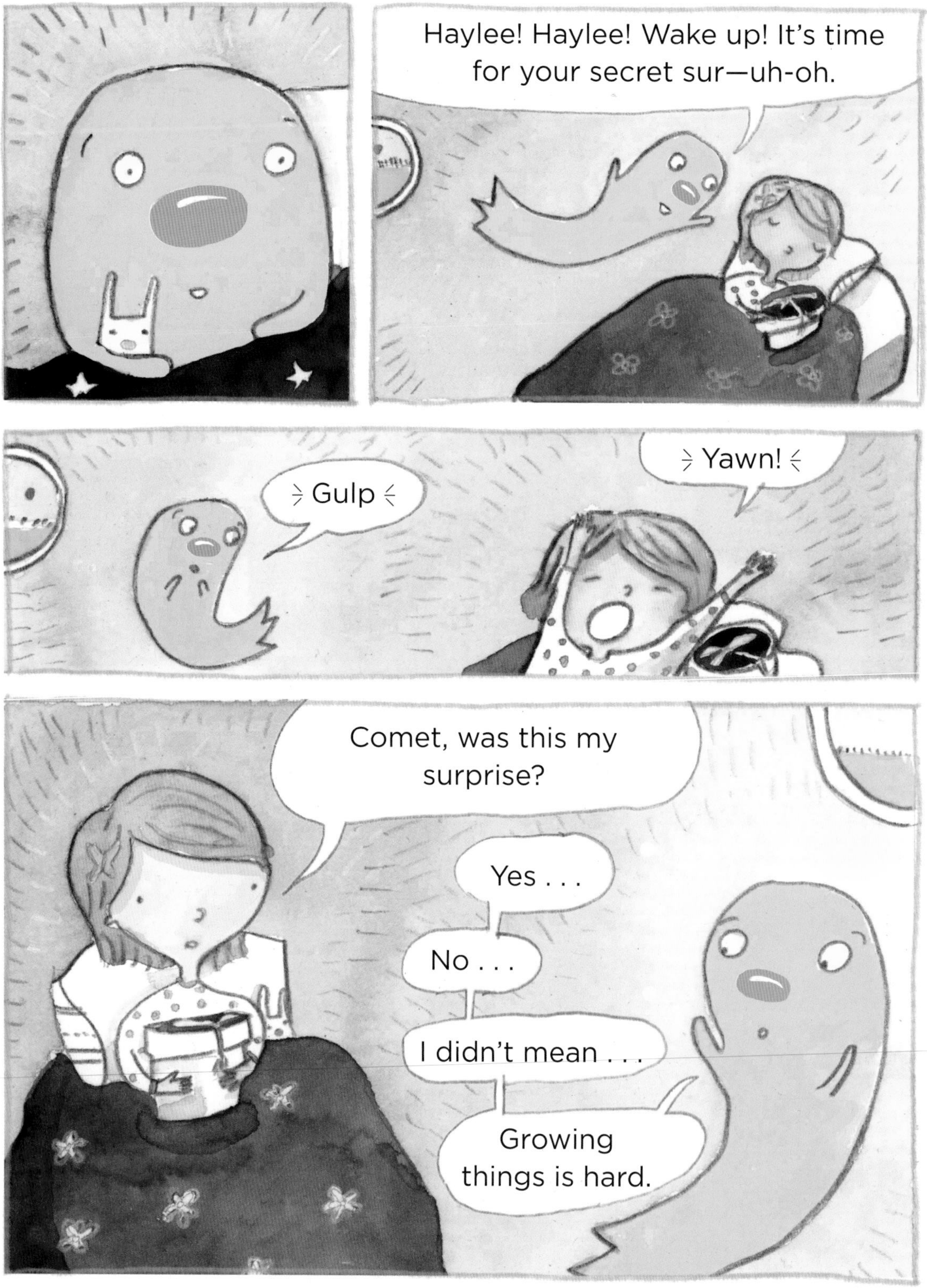
Haylee! Haylee! Wake up! It's time for your secret sur—uh-oh.
Gulp
Yawn!
Comet, was this my surprise?
Yes . . .
No . . .
I didn't mean . . .
Growing things is hard.

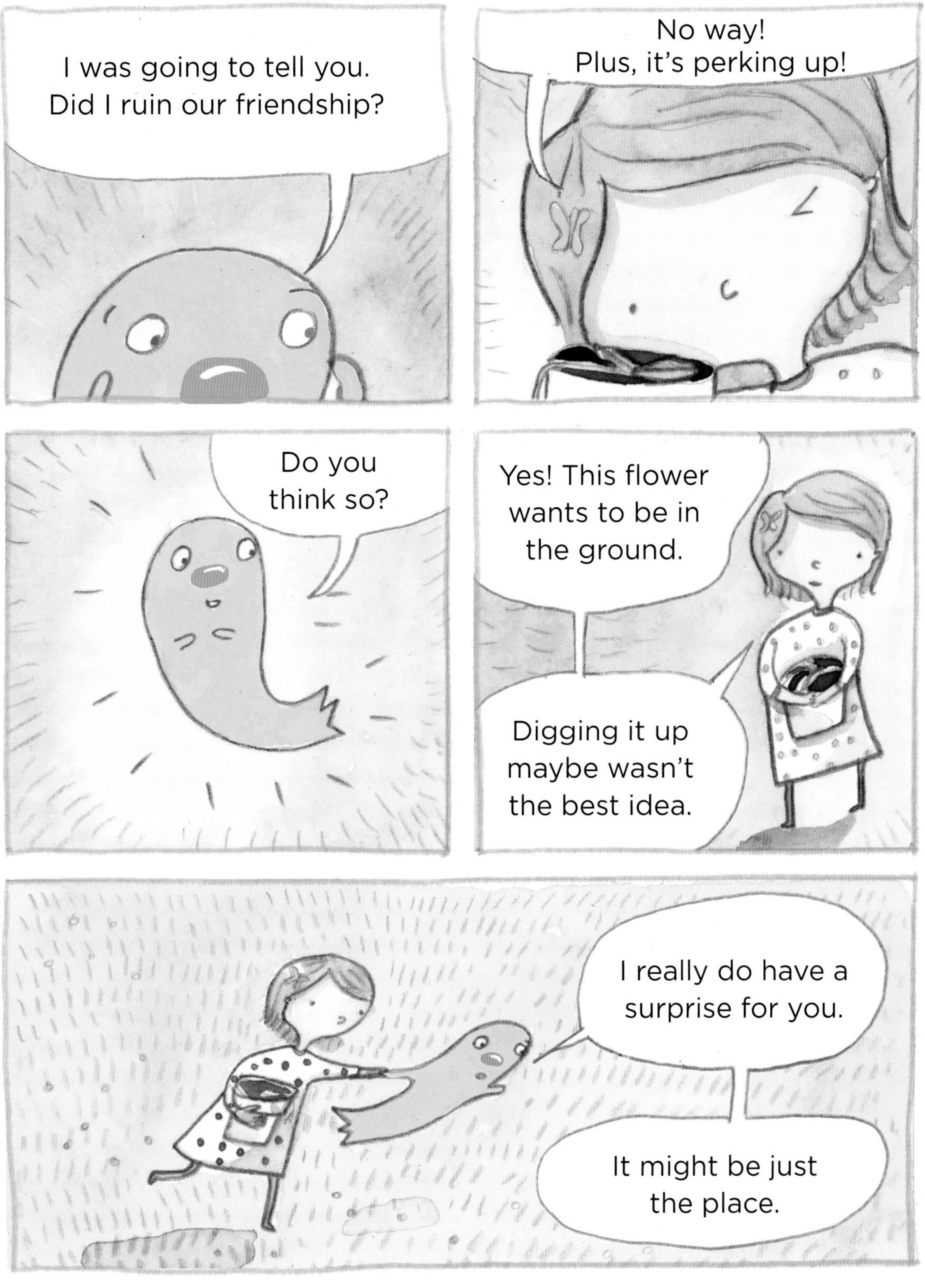
I was going to tell you. Did I ruin our friendship?
No way! Plus, it's perking up!
Do you think so?
Yes! This flower wants to be in the ground.
Digging it up maybe wasn't the best idea.
I really do have a surprise for you.
It might be just the place.

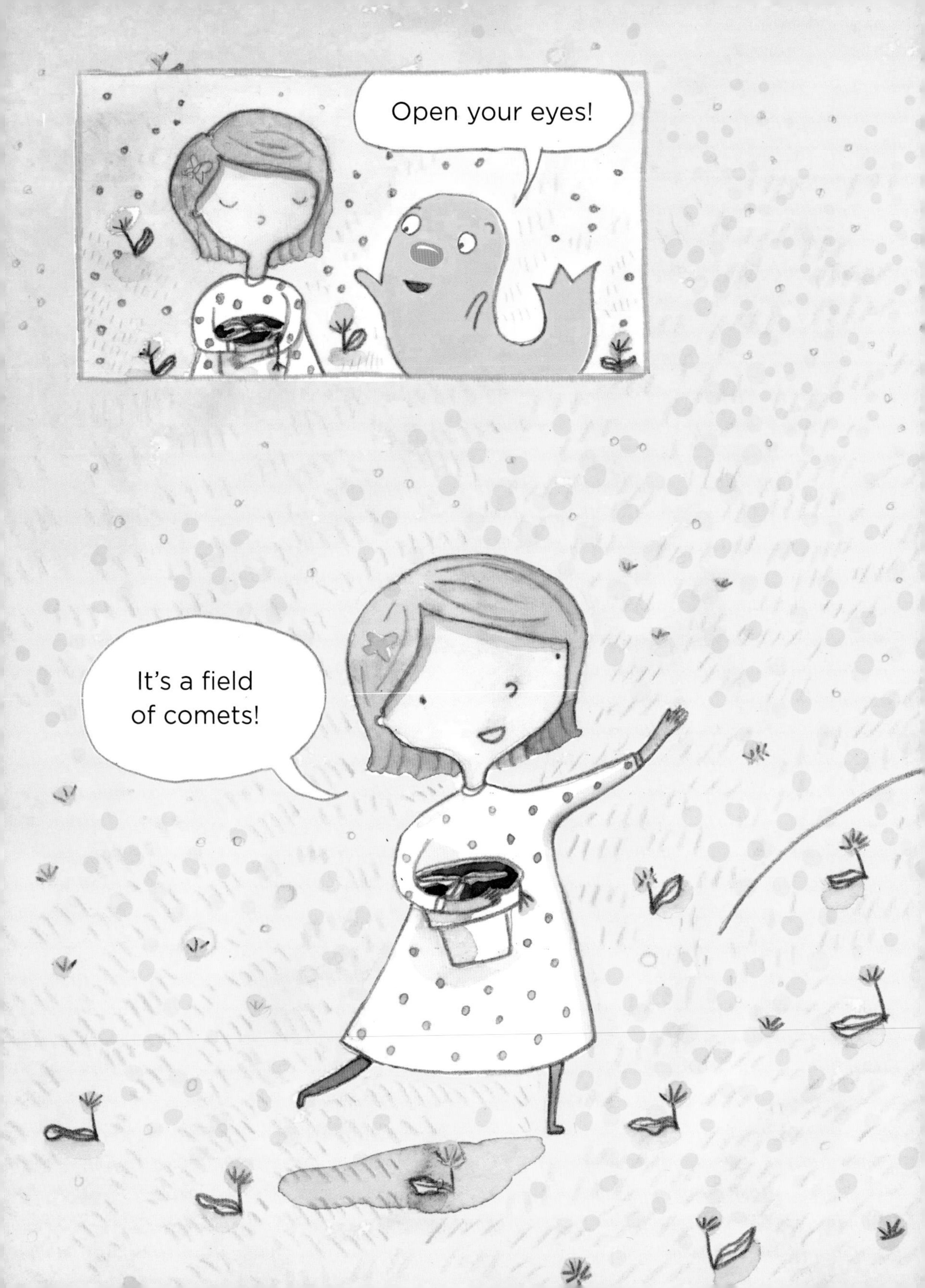
Open your eyes!
It’s a field of comets!

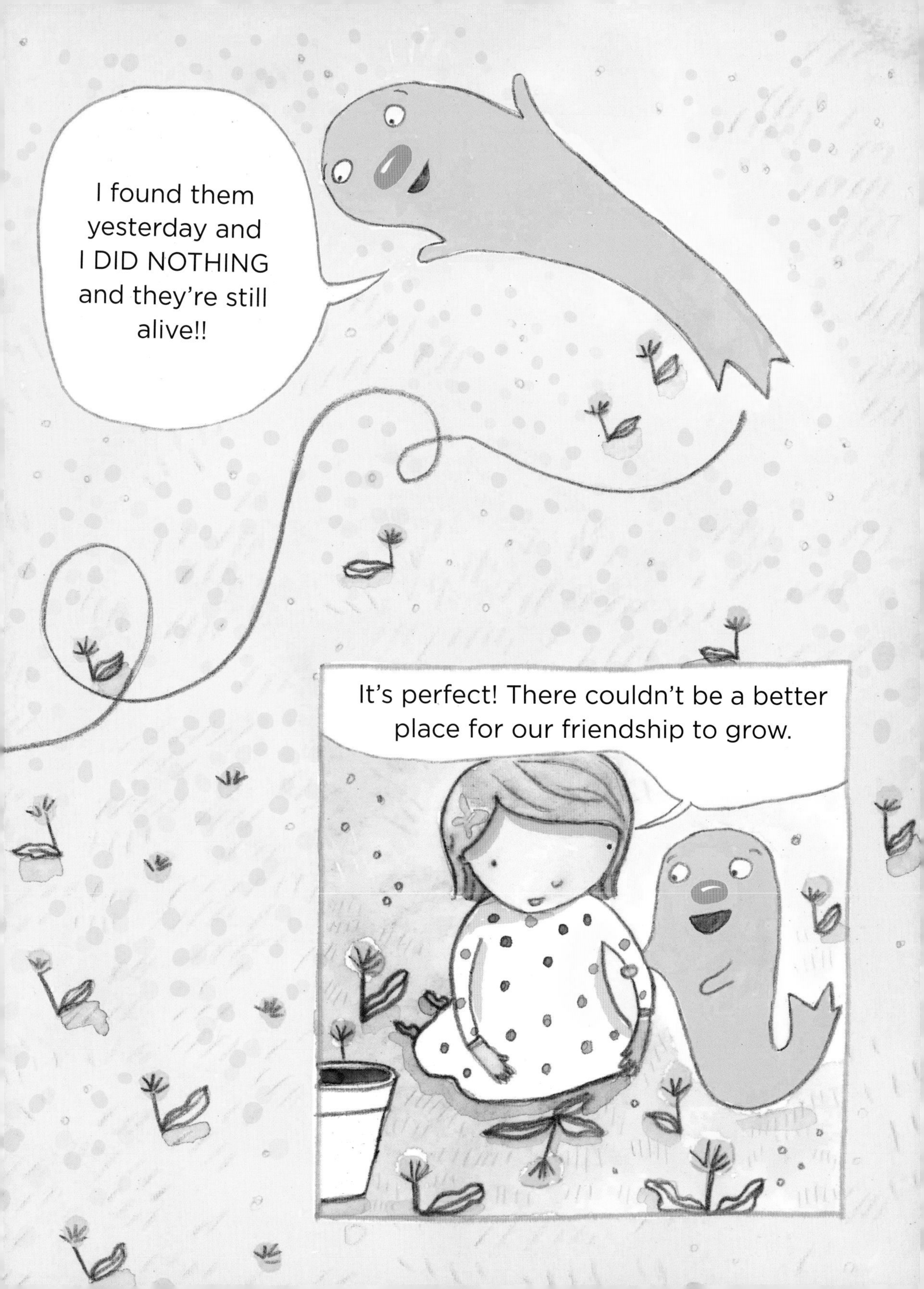
I found them yesterday and I DID NOTHING and they're still alive!!
It's perfect! There couldn't be a better place for our friendship to grow.

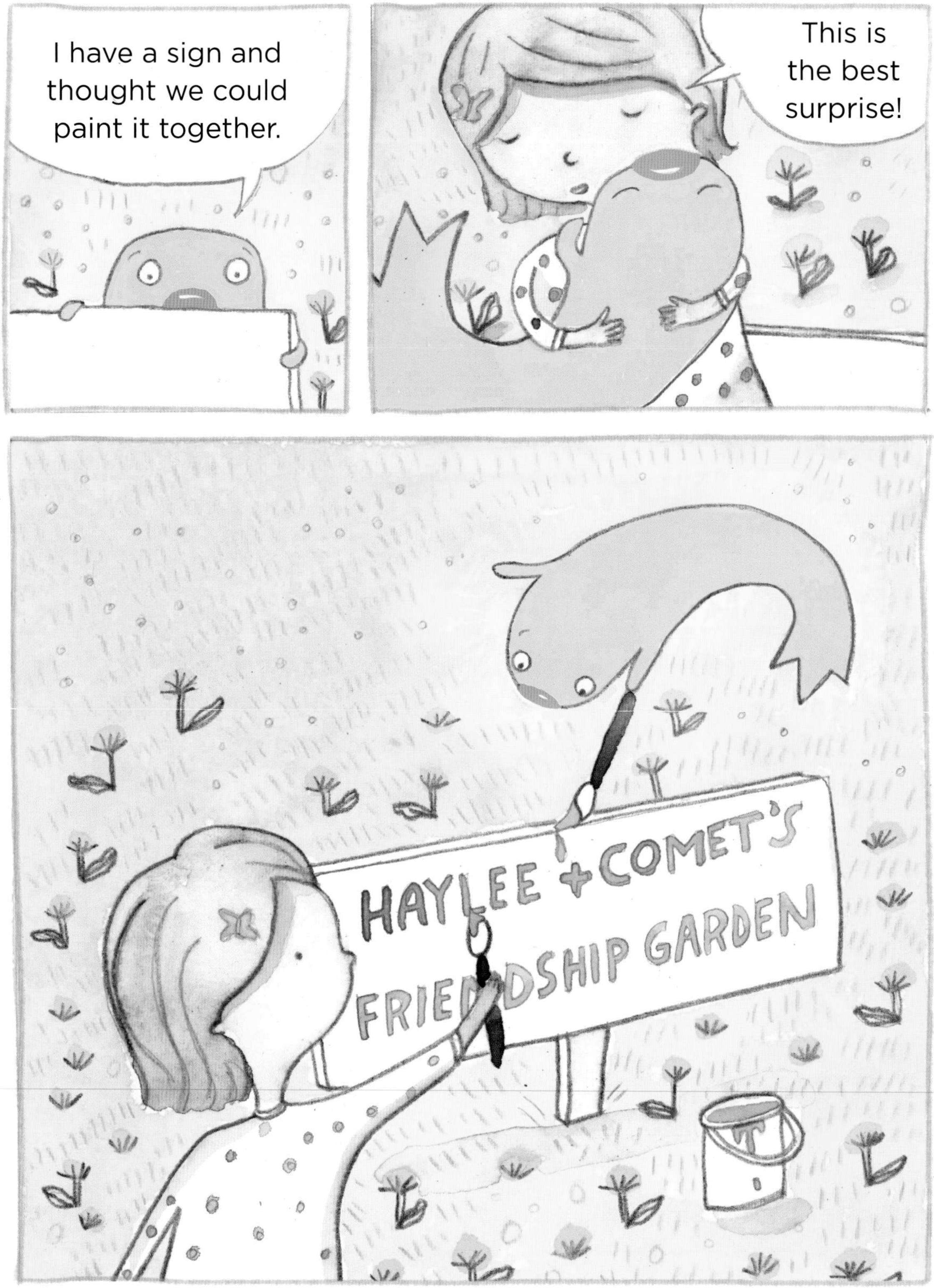
I have a sign and thought we could paint it together.
This is the best surprise!
HAYLEE + COMET'S FRIENDSHIP GARDEN

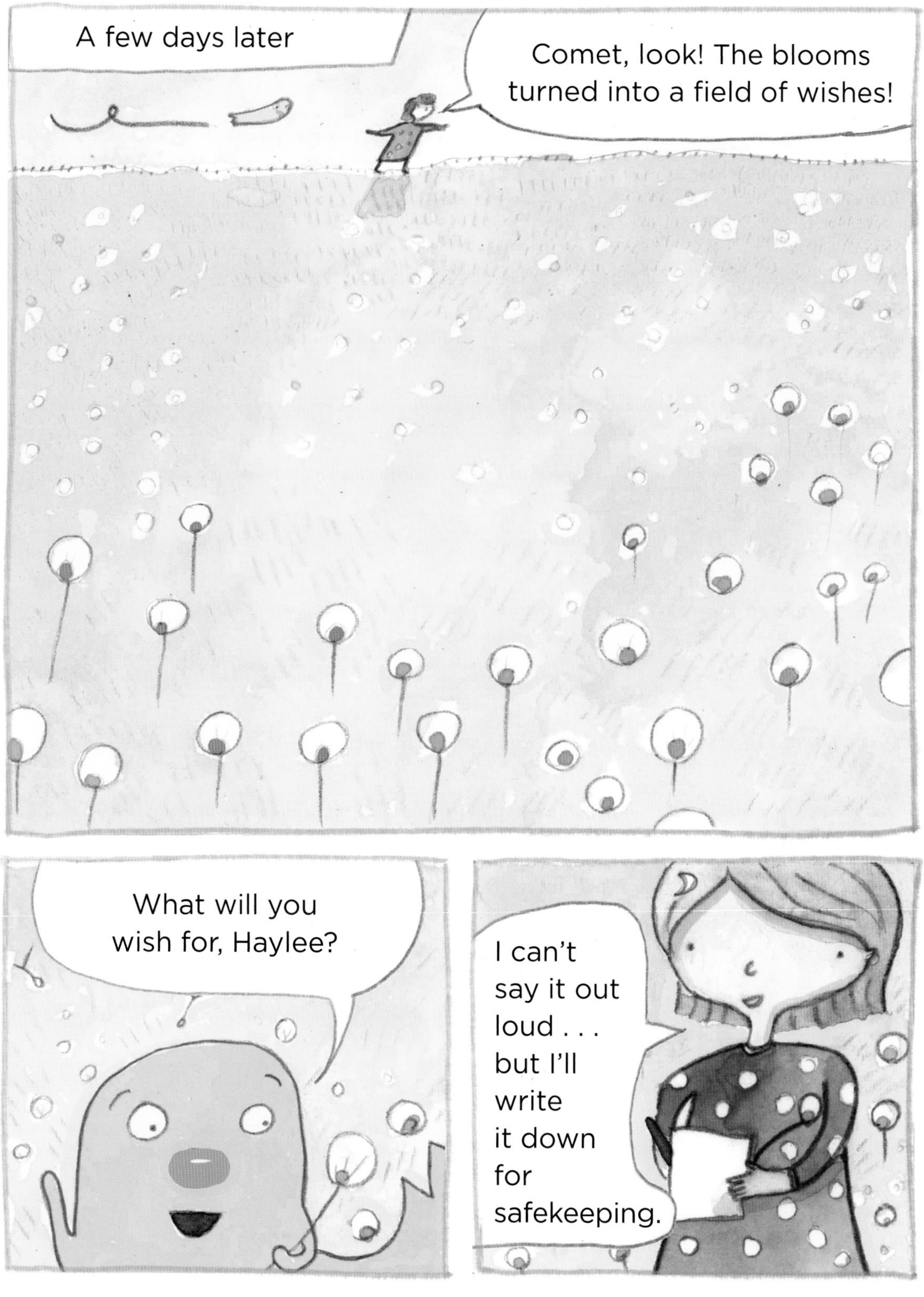
A few days later
Comet, look! The blooms turned into a field of wishes!
What will you wish for, Haylee?
I can't say it out loud . . . but I'll write it down for safekeeping.

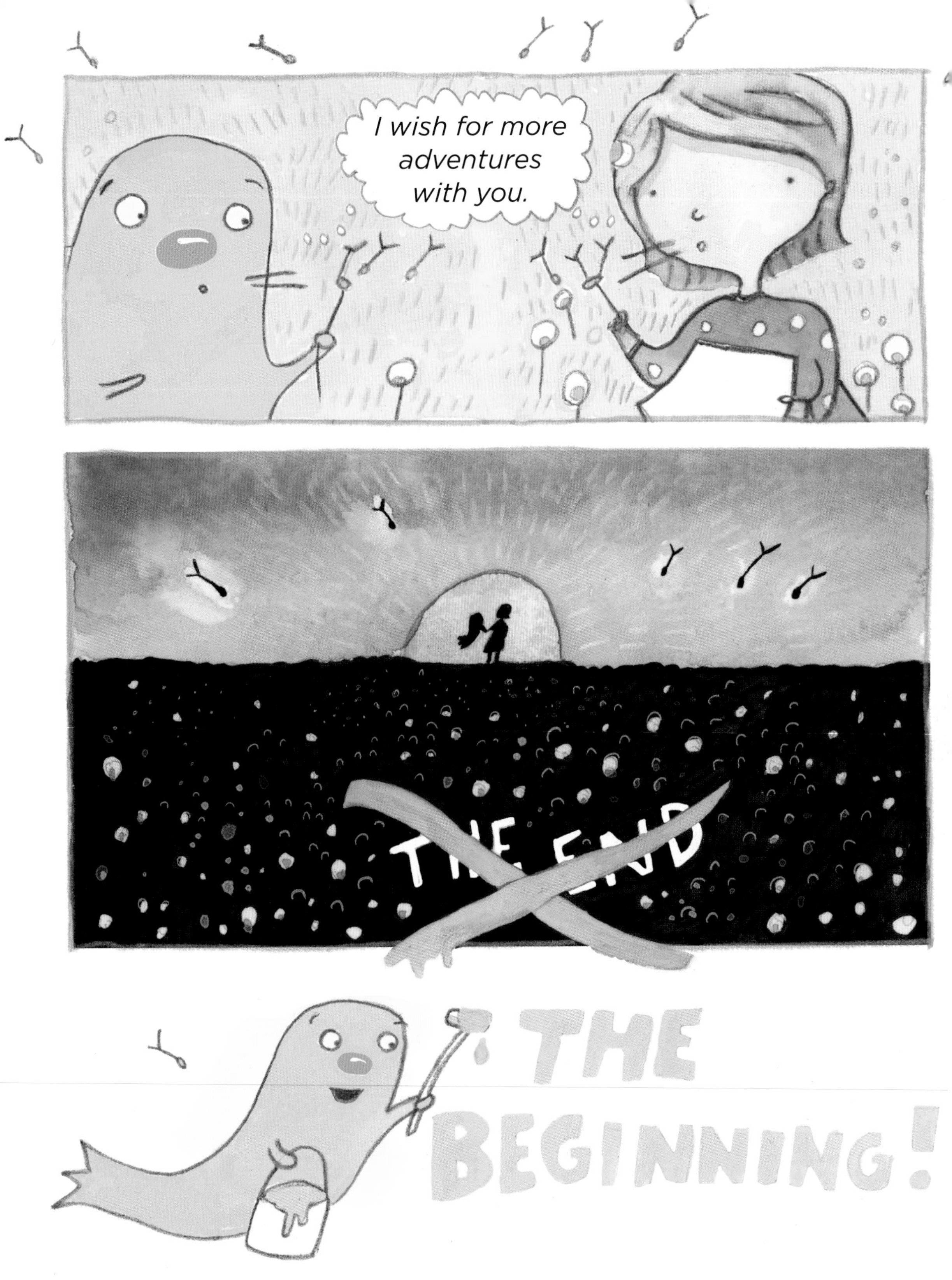
I wish for more adventures with you.
THE END
THE BEGINNING!

Wishes for future adventures:

Canoeing

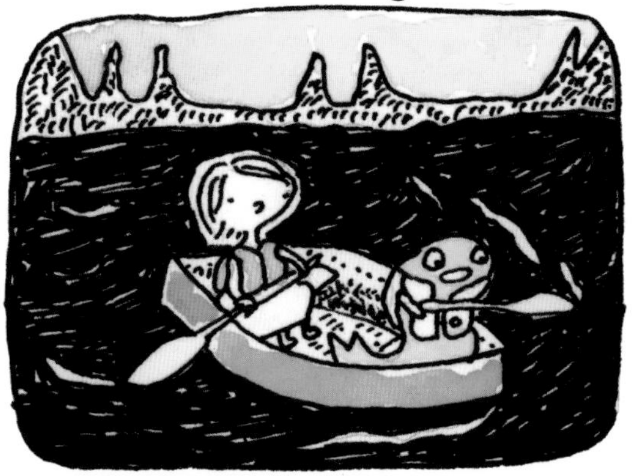

Biking

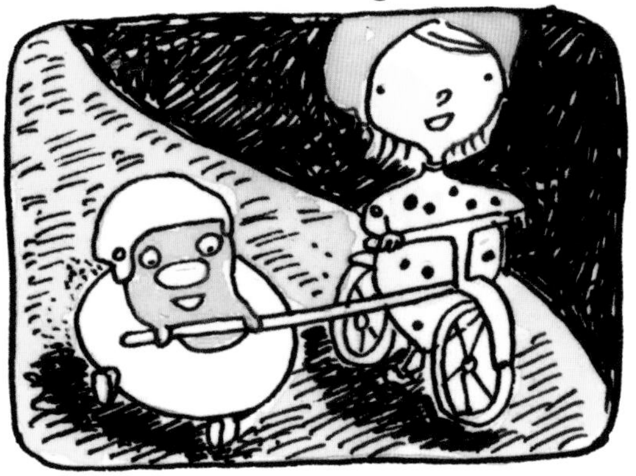

Cocoon Watching

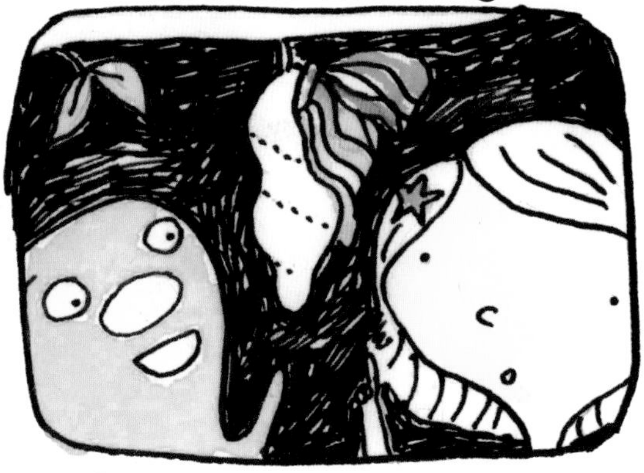

Snow Cone Eating

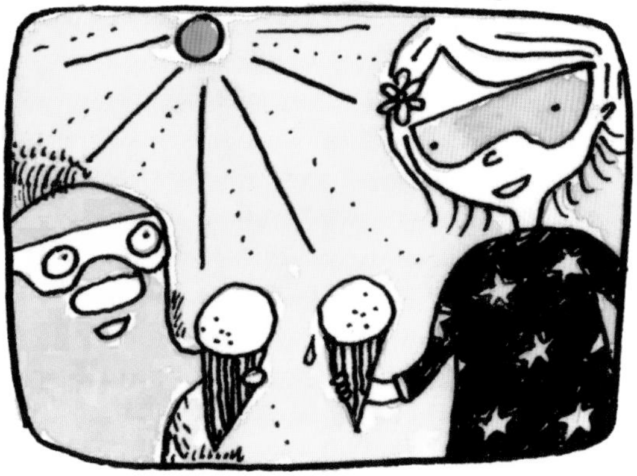

Camping

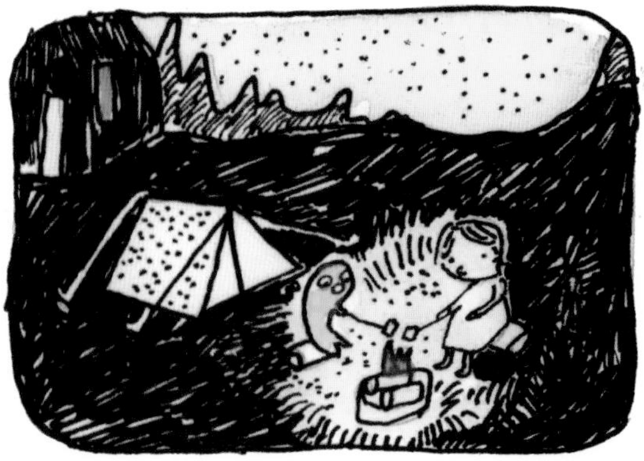

Firefly Catching

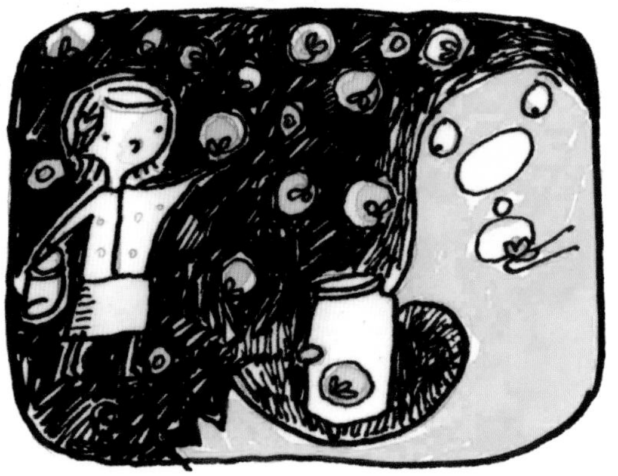

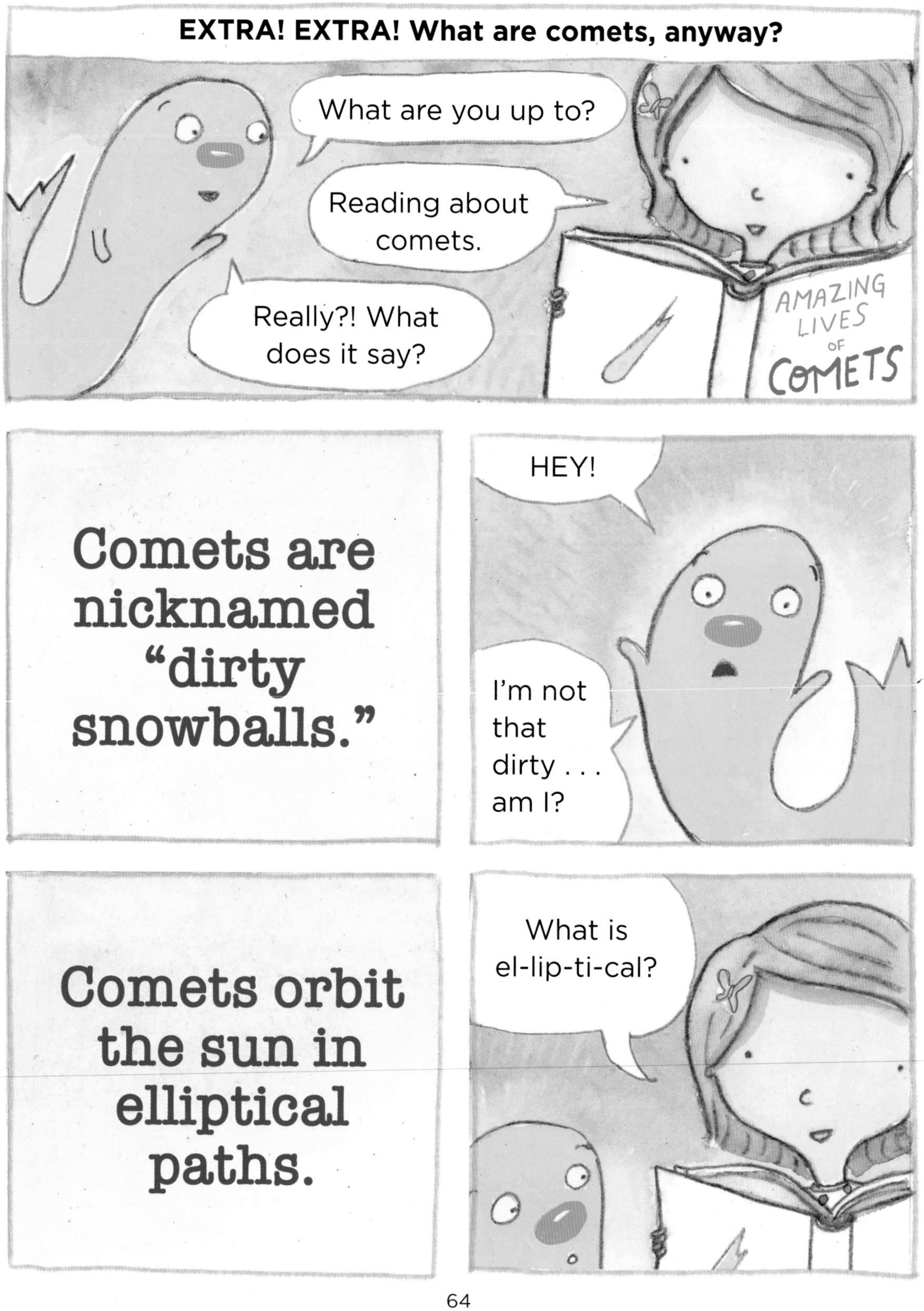
EXTRA! EXTRA! What are comets, anyway?
What are you up to?
Reading about comets.
Really?! What does it say?
AMAZING LIVES OF COMETS
Comets are nicknamed "dirty snowballs."
HEY!
I'm not that dirty . . . am I?
Comets orbit the sun in elliptical paths.
What is el-lip-ti-cal?

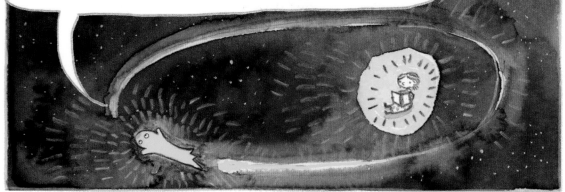

If you are the sun and I am the comet, my path is like an oval or a stretched-out circle.

Halley's Comet is the most famous comet, and it's visible about every 75 years.

Halley, like you?

Close! Halley rhymes with "valley." It's named after Edmond Halley, a British astronomer born in 1656.

I don't need to be famous.

Me neither. Just important to someone.

Haylee, who rhymes with "daily," you are important to me.

And you, dear Comet, are the most important comet to me. And I get to see you every day!

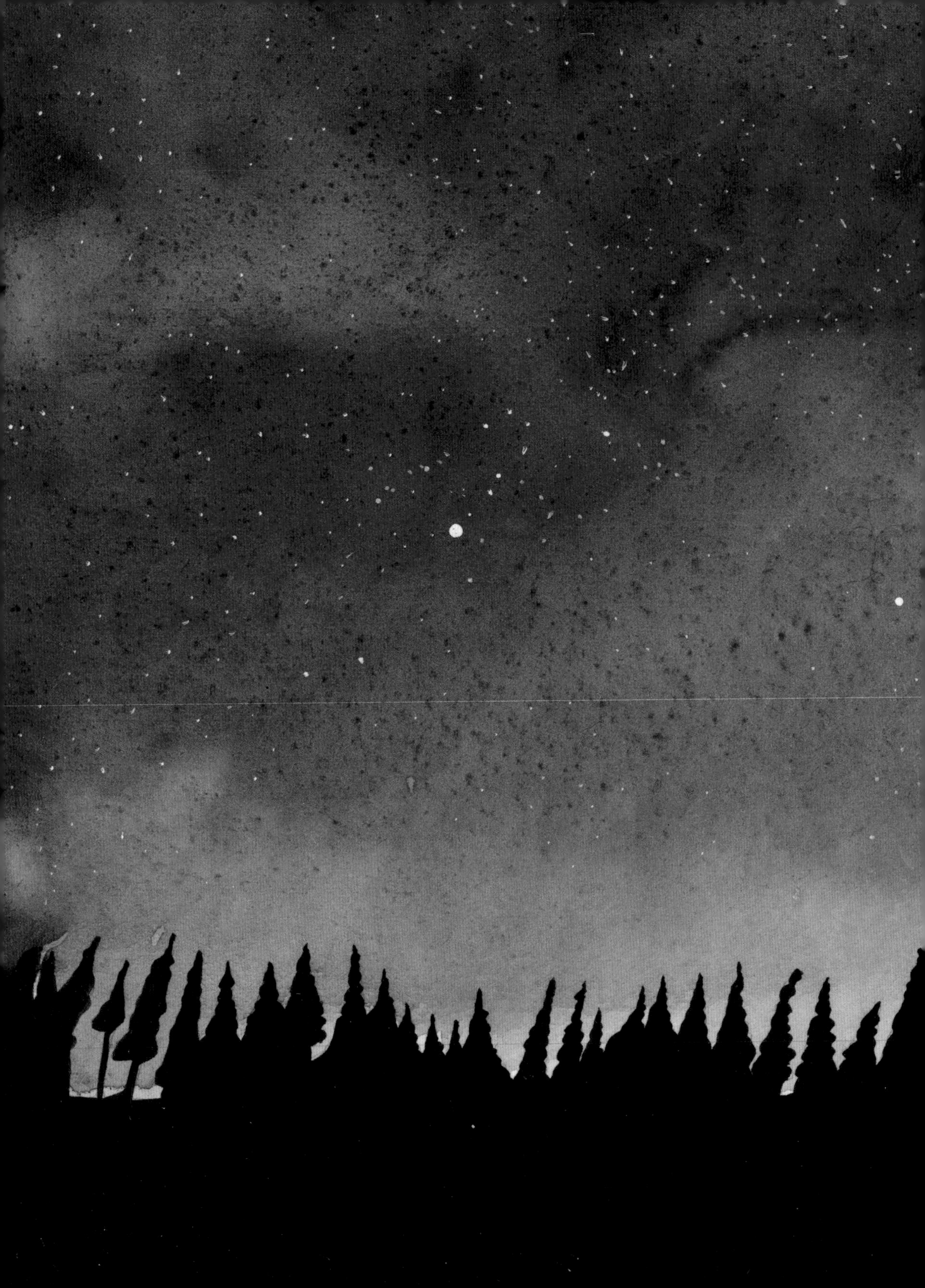